IT'S HER FAULT

An aging university professor insists to Detective Frank Vandegraf that his estranged wife is trying to kill him, but the problem is that she's nowhere to be found. A relative claims that it's the other way around: the husband is actually threatening to kill his wife. When the professor turns up murdered shortly thereafter, with a mysterious note lying on his chest that says 'IT'S HER FAULT', Frank redoubles his efforts to locate the missing wife, his prime suspect. But when he does, the case becomes even more baffling . . .

Books by Tony Gleeson
in the Linford Mystery Library:

NIGHT MUSIC

TONY GLEESON

◆

IT'S HER FAULT

Complete and Unabridged

LINFORD
Leicester

First published in Great Britain

First Linford Edition
published 2016

A catalogue record for this book is available
from the British Library.

ISBN 978–1–4448–2843–6

Published by
F. A. Thorpe (Publishing)
Anstey, Leicestershire

Set by Words & Graphics Ltd.
Anstey, Leicestershire
Printed and bound in Great Britain by
T. J. International Ltd., Padstow, Cornwall

This book is printed on acid-free paper

DEDICATION:
To Annie, who inspired it all

1

It all began when Marlon Morrison refused to abandon his meatball marinara sandwich.

'Hey Frank,' he called across his desk. 'Do me a favor and take this call for me?' Even as he plunged the meatball hero into his gaping mouth with his left hand, he held out a pink phone slip with his other.

It was not surprising to Frank Vandegraf that his colleague, Detective Morrison, would be attempting to pass off still another chore to someone else. There was a running joke in the Personal Crimes Unit that Morrison, when thanked for some favor or other, was fond of saying 'It was the very least I could do' — and that was absolutely what he always did, the very least he could.

Frank, who had been trying to walk past Marlon's desk without calling attention to himself, sighed resignedly and

1

reached out for the slip. What the hell, he figured. He was, if not free, at least relatively unencumbered at the moment, as much as anybody in the unit ever was. Why not.

'Some professor says his wife is trying to kill him,' Morrison mumbled with a mouth full of meatball.

Frank gave the phone slip a quick scan.

'Somewhere up in the hills,' Morrison added before taking another bite. 'I owe you one, Frank,' he called to Frank's back as he departed. Marlon owed a lot of guys one. He owed most of them more than one. Frank wasn't going to hold his breath waiting to get reimbursed.

★ ★ ★

The hills that rose along the eastern side of the city were a ten-minute drive from the station, which no doubt accounted further for Marlon's reluctance to take the call, but it was also a nice jaunt through some of the better neighborhoods. Frank judged that he could use a little cheering up, so he was actually whistling as he grabbed his car keys from his desk and headed out the door.

Developers had taken full advantage of the views afforded from the hillside to the harbor and coast off to the west. Further to the north, as the hills got higher, were expensive one-family hillside homes, but Frank's destination was the condominium district, where a line of identical trendily designed buildings rose into the sky. The district had been officially named Scenic Hills by the developers, but the name had never stuck, and most still simply referred to the area as the Hills.

Professor Maurice Hesterberg lived near the top floor of such a building. 'Thank you for coming, Detective Vandegraf,' Hesterberg was saying as he sat next to him on his balcony. It was a glorious sunny day, a good breeze making the air crystal clear, and they could see the ocean in the distance right to the horizon. He rattled the ice cubes in his glass of iced tea. 'You're sure I can't get you something?'

'Thanks, no,' Frank replied. He had pulled a beat-up notebook out of his pocket and opened it to the next available page. 'Now tell me, Mr. Hesterberg — '

'Doctor,' Hesterberg interrupted.

'Excuse me?'

'That's Dr. Hesterberg.'

'Dr. Hesterberg. All right.'

'I know — it seems pretentious, doesn't it?' He spoke in a clipped but precise manner, more than a little fussy and self-conscious. Frank could see it was going to get annoying soon enough.

'Not a problem, Doctor. Now — '

'But, you see, I worked damned hard to earn that title. While I was working on my master's and PhD, I also worked full-time as an electrician.'

'You did?'

'Crawled around under houses, in between walls. Got shocked more than a few times. Fell out of a few houses. Not an easy way to get through school.'

It did not sound, Frank reflected silently, that the doctor was very good at being an electrician. Probably a good thing he had gone into academia.

'So you see, I kind of feel I deserve that title of respect. Sometimes people tell me they think only medical doctors deserve to be called Doctor. I tell them, respectfully, that that's rubbish.'

Respectfully indeed, Frank reflected. 'Whatever you say, Dr. Hesterberg. I have no trouble with calling you that. Now you called saying you think someone is trying to kill you?'

'That's correct — my wife. My *estranged* wife, to be precise.'

Which explained, Frank mused, why so far there seemed no sign of a female presence in this condo. Of course he couldn't have unerringly made that judgment without having yet seen the bedroom and the bathroom, but a detective of a certain number of years just picked up on some things intuitively.

'Your wife doesn't live here then, sir?'

'No, we've been separated for some time now. She lives in an apartment on the other side of town.'

'Your wife's name is . . . ?'

'Margo. Margo Hesterberg. We are still officially married.' Hesterberg sighed deeply, looking out at the view. 'Hopefully not for too much longer.'

'So tell me, why do you think Margo is trying to kill you, uh, Doctor?'

'Well, for one thing, she poisoned my dog. For another thing, she's threatened me. And she's tried to break into my condominium.'

'Poisoned your dog?'

'Yes. I found my Schnauzer, Thomas Mann, dead one evening when I returned home. Lying there by his food dish, by the kitchen window over there, under those Venetian blinds.' He pointed through the open balcony door into the apartment.

'Thomas Mann?'

'That was his name, yes. After the German novelist.'

'I've heard of him, thank you. Wrote *Death in Venice*, I believe?' Frank resisted the urge to pursue the apparent irony any further.

'I am suitably impressed, Detective. You're a reader, then.'

Frank waved a hand. 'He was poisoned, you're sure? The dog, I mean, not the writer.'

'My veterinarian did an autopsy and confirmed it. I also brought the food dish to him and he found traces of rat poison in it.'

'So someone had come into your home and left poison for Thomas — I mean, your dog.'

'Yes.' Hesterberg nodded vigorously, his jaw set. 'I duly reported it to the police, but no action was ever taken.'

Frank scribbled rapidly into his notebook. 'You feel this was done by your wife, and it was part of an ongoing threat directed at you.'

'No question in my mind about it.'

'And why do you feel it was your wife who broke into your home and killed your dog?'

'Because she hated him. She said I loved Thomas Mann more than I did her.'

'There were signs of her breaking in? Something to lead you to conclude it had to be her?'

'There were no such signs. She had to have a key.'

'To your knowledge, did she have a key?'

'No. I changed the locks when she left. But somehow she must have gotten one.'

'Let's come back to that in a moment, Doctor. Tell me some more about the perceived threats Margo made on your life.'

'She would call me at all hours of the night, wake me up, and rave at me. Accuse me of all sorts of bizarre perfidy. More than once she said she was going to make sure I couldn't cause her any more trouble.'

'Trouble?'

'Yes, that was the word she used: 'trouble.' Several times she said that.'

'What *kind* of trouble did she think you were causing her?'

Hesterberg shrugged and dramatically opened his eyes wide. He had thick, dark, wiry eyebrows and a beard to match. Combined with his self-conscious manner, the effect was heavy on the drama. 'I never got that straight, Detective. She was increasingly irrational. All I know is that she made clear-cut threats to my well-being in her late-night telephone rants.'

'Is there any record of these calls? Did you happen to record any of these, for example?'

'My God no,' Hesterberg replied. 'Now I wish I had taken steps to do so.'

'Did your wife specifically and expressly say she was going to try to kill you?'

Hesterberg shook his head in frustration. 'I can't recall specifically, no, but her meaning was clear.'

'She said, maybe, she was going to take you out? Remove you from the scene? Eliminate you? Something like that?'

'Conceivably. I don't remember exactly. The woman has been irrational.'

'Did these calls start before or after you found your dog poisoned?'

Hesterberg considered this. 'It was around the same time. I believe she began disturbing me just before I found poor Thomas Mann's body.'

'Did you confront her with this, ask her if she had done it?'

'One night I did, yes. She did not confirm it, but neither did she deny it outright. Rather, she laughed. The night conversations were unhinged, you have to understand; very disturbing. They were not the most coherent. I have to admit I found myself drawn into her madness and often responded emotionally. Not to mention, she always woke me, so I wasn't at my best to begin with.'

'When did you last speak with your wife, Doctor?'

'It's been a few days now. Two or three. She hasn't called. There's been no word or contact from her. That's why I'm really worried now.'

Frank paused in his writing and looked up. 'Excuse me? You're really worried now because . . . ?'

'It's the calm before the storm, of course,' Hesterberg intoned dramatically. 'She's stopped calling me because she's up to something. I can feel it. So I knew it was time to call the police.'

The remainder of the interview was not much more helpful. Frank ascertained that Hesterberg had been a tenured English professor at the nearby State University for many years, and even headed the department for a while. At age sixty-five he was currently semi-retired, not wanting to totally give up his life's work, teaching only two full-time upper-division courses and acting as advisor for a doctoral candidate. The rest of his time was devoted to a book he was writing on twentieth-century German literary movements, and apparently to long walks and an occasional visit to a local bar for a few cognacs with one or two fellow academics. He and Margo had been married for about a quarter of a century and had, in his words, grown increasingly apart from one another over the past few years.

Hesterberg attributed much of their marital discord to what he termed Margo's ongoing 'descent into madness' — becoming ever more paranoid, suspicious, and withdrawn. She was, he said, jealous of any time or energy he spent with anyone or anything else. She suspected his tavern companions, his long walks, even his dog. He did have to admit, she had never once committed a violent act or even shown any tendencies to violence. But she had grown increasingly emotional and irrational.

Finally the confrontation had erupted that resulted in her deciding to leave. She had rented an apartment near her sister, her last surviving relative. Hesterberg figured that once a divorce had been effected, they would sell the condo, which was still joint property, and divide the proceeds.

Frank wondered why Margo had left rather than Hesterberg himself. It was explained that she had made that judgment herself; she wanted nothing more to do with the place where they had spent so much time together. The memories, she said, were not pleasant.

'So let me make sure I've got the actual facts here straight,' Frank was summing up as he prepared to leave, tucking his notebook into his inner sports coat pocket. 'You suspect that your wife plans to kill you. She has made no specific statement to that effect, to you or to anyone else in your knowledge. You believe she entered your condo illicitly and poisoned your dog, but you have no concrete proof of either of these things.'

'My feelings are strong on this, Detective. I am totally convinced it's her and that that is her plan, yes.' Hesterberg seemed to see no difficulty in this view. 'So what are you going to do about it?'

'I'm afraid my options are a bit limited legally here, sir. Frankly, your feelings by themselves are not much of a basis for action. I'm going to go have a talk with your wife for starters. Then I'll see where that takes me.'

'Are you going to provide me police protection?' Hesterberg demanded.

Frank rubbed the back of his neck. 'I don't know that I've got enough evidence to be able to get that for you, but I'll look into it. If there was just something more clear-cut . . . '

'She's a deranged woman. I've never known her to be specifically violent, I told you that, but there's something different about her of late. She's become frighteningly unpredictable. I'm absolutely convinced she is dangerous.'

* * *

The address Frank had been given for Margo was an older but still highly respectable neighborhood, where brick predominated: four- and five-story apartment buildings and some two- and three-story row houses

13

along tree-lined streets. There were actually people on the streets, walking dogs, riding bikes. Kids were playing. Frank considered that he would have opted for a neighborhood like this over the condos any time.

Margo lived in a garden apartment to the rear in a low building. Frank rang the number on the intercom several times but received no answer. Finally he rang the on-premises superintendent, who luckily was home and buzzed him in. Another nice perk, he mused, of an older neighborhood like this one.

The building was tended by a husband and wife who lived in the basement; the wife happened to be the one who was present to greet Frank. She was a robust, no-nonsense type, maybe fifty, in slacks and sweatshirt, who stood at her open door with her arms crossed as Frank produced his badge and ID and mentioned the garden apartment.

'Looking for Miz Hesterberg,' she observed.

'Yes, ma'am. She isn't answering the bell. Have you seen her recently?'

'Can't say as I have,' Super Lady replied. 'What's this about?'

'Just routine. I need to talk with her. Any idea when she might be home?'

'She usually *is* home. Doesn't go out all that much, maybe to do shopping or visit her sister down the street.'

'Any chance she's home and just not answering the bell?'

Super Lady shrugged. 'You're welcome to go knock on her door and see.'

Frank did just that, hiking up the steps and down the hall to the rear apartment. He knocked several times and called out, 'Mrs. Hesterberg?' But there was no reply. He went back to the superintendents' apartment and knocked on the door. Super Lady threw it open.

'If we're going to get to be this friendly,' she said dryly, 'you might as well know my name's Judy.'

'Sorry to bother you again, uh, Judy. I was just wondering if you know Margo's sister, her name, maybe her exact address?'

'Her sister's name is Monica. She lives around the corner.' She rattled off an address. Frank fumbled for a pencil and his notebook and wrote it down, thanked her and departed.

Monica Wersching did indeed happen to be at home; she lived in a brick row house, aging but well-maintained, with a cement stoop leading up to the entrance. She promptly answered the doorbell and after inspecting his credentials, invited Frank in.

'So this is about Margo,' she said as she led him into a front parlor and motioned for him to have a seat. 'Are you finally going to do something, then?'

'Ma'am, excuse me?' Frank said as he sat down in a comfortable leather chair. She sat across from him on her sofa.

'About her husband. About the threats.'

The sister apparently knew about the threats? This was interesting but confusing. 'Maybe you better tell me what you're referring to?' He didn't take out his notebook yet, just leaned forward, forearms across his thighs, fingers laced, and stared intently.

'Did she finally contact you, as I've been urging her to do for some time now?'

'No, ma'am. Contact me about what, exactly?'

Monica was a lean, serious-looking woman perhaps in her late 50s. She returned Frank's gaze earnestly. 'About the threats, of course! From Max!'

'Max? Who's Max?'

Now Monica was getting irritated. 'Her *husband! Max!*'

'You mean Maurice? Maurice Hesterberg?'

'Yes. She always called him Max. Tell me that's why you're here. Please tell me.'

'You're telling me that Margo has been receiving threats from her husband, Dr. Hesterberg?'

'And you're telling me that's not why you're here, Detective?' Now Monica looked really perturbed. 'So tell me, why are you here, then?'

Frank took a deep breath and decided to start over.

★ ★ ★

He listened, now with his notebook and pencil in hand, as Monica told him the stories her younger sister Margo had shared with her about odd and alarming behavior on the part of her husband since she had moved out. When she had first found the garden apartment, she had been delighted. She could walk out her back door into a small verdant paradise with a canopy of trees, full bushes, lovely pots of flowers, and a charming stone walk, all sheltered by ivy-covered brick walls.

Since the incidents, she was terrified to be living on a ground floor and was actively searching for a new apartment several stories off the ground with less access to unwanted intruders. She was convinced that her husband had broken into her place several times and had performed what she termed 'subtle vandalism' of various sorts.

'She would find things broken,' Monica said. 'Or missing. Or, most strangely of all, mysteriously misplaced, from one location to another inside the apartment. She was sure it was Max — that he was 'gaslighting' her, as she liked to call it. Are you familiar with that old movie, Detective?'

'A bit before my time, but yes, I've seen

it. Ingrid Bergman and Charles Boyer. A classic from the forties. I get her reference. He was trying to convince her she was going mad by manipulating things.'

'Margo is quite the film buff. She tells me she prefers the earlier British version, actually. But that's neither here nor there. You understand my point.'

'Margo thinks her husband is trying to drive her crazy — or at least make her appear that she's crazy, is that what you're saying?'

'Exactly. She was hesitant to contact the police because she was sure that's just what you *would* think.'

Frank caught himself rubbing the back of his neck. He had to stop this habit. Several people had told him that he did it constantly. 'Mrs. Wersching . . .'

'It's Ms. now, actually,' she interrupted. 'I'm not partial to being called 'Miss.' My husband passed away some years ago, and I readopted my original family name.'

'I'm sorry, Ms. Wersching. I've actually been told that Margo has tended to be a little, well, over-stressed of late and perhaps unduly suspicious. Is it possible that — '

'That she's imagining things? That she's paranoid? Is that why you're here, Detective Vanderbilt?'

'Vandegraf actually,' Frank corrected. This was not productive. 'Listen, I think I need to speak with Margo herself, directly. She doesn't seem to be at home right now. Do you have any idea when would be a good time for me to catch her?'

'I don't know; I haven't spoken with her in a couple of days myself. She spends a lot of time at home, in her garden. At least she used to. Lately she locks her doors and windows and sits inside and reads or watches DVDs of old films. Let me give her a call.' She got up and walked to a cordless phone on a nearby table. A lot of people were giving up their land lines nowadays, Frank mused. At home, he still liked keeping his.

Monica dialed and waited. Apparently an answering machine or voice mail picked up because she left a short message for Margo to call her back. She hit the OFF button and turned to Frank with a shrug. 'No idea where she might be,' she said. 'I'll let you know if I hear from her.'

Frank stood up and handed her one of his cards, then stopped and sat back down. He asked for, and jotted down, her own phone number. 'If you don't mind, can I just ask you a few questions about Margo?'

Monica looked somewhat less friendly than she had only shortly before, but she relented and sat down. 'Such as?'

'Can you tell me about her marriage to Max — I mean Dr. Hesterberg?'

'She met him when she was a grad student and he was her faculty advisor. He was a rather dashing and romantic sort in those days. He was brilliant and mature, well-traveled and experienced, but he embraced a very youthful lifestyle, the way he dressed and talked, the music he listened to. He was very open to the younger culture, loved his students, went drinking with them — probably smoked pot with them too, is my guess. She was considerably his junior in years, of course

— maybe fifteen years; naïve and idealistic. Not surprising she became infatuated with him and fell in love.'

'They got married what, twenty years ago?'

'Twenty-five, to be exact. He basically swept her off her feet. She was quite beautiful, full of the love of life. I could see why he was attracted to her. They seemed very happy in those early years.'

'You're saying they became less happy with time?'

'Gradually, don't people always?'

'I don't know if I'm quite that cynical,' Frank allowed, still writing. 'But yes, married people do sometimes get disenchanted. But your point is that the marriage was no longer idyllic?'

'More so in recent years. Margo seemed very disturbed by something that was going on. She made comments about finding out that Max wasn't precisely what she had thought he was.'

'Any idea what she meant by that?'

'Oh, I pressed her, but she remained cryptic. Wouldn't tell me details.'

'Is it possible her husband was having

some kind of affair, something like that?'

Monica shrugged slightly. 'I never knew or heard of anything like that. Max had settled down after meeting Margo. He seemed to grow up, be more serious. Seemed more interested in his work than, say, in other women. I suppose it's not out of the question. Such things do happen as men grow older and happen to notice their wives are doing the same, don't they?' She smiled, saw Frank was not going to rise to the bait, and moved on. 'I don't entirely know what Margo meant when she started telling me Max wasn't what she had thought he was. She wouldn't elaborate.'

'When did she first start telling you things like that?'

Monica thought about that for a while before replying. 'Maybe three years ago was when she really began to get agitated.'

'Ms. Wersching, please don't take this the wrong way. I have to consider every possibility here. Is it possible your sister was becoming . . . disturbed in some way; that she was believing things were

23

happening that might not have been?'

That took Monica aback, and she shot Frank a glare before regaining her composure. 'You mean was she going crazy, imagining things? Is that what you're asking?'

'As I said, I've got to consider every possibility here. I don't know any of you.'

'Trying to be as fair as I can with you, Detective, Margo was getting more and more . . . disconcerted, shall we say, on a daily basis the past few years. She was clearly emotionally upset and progressively allowing it to affect her in a worse way. I can't discount that that might have colored her perceptions of things. In fact, I was very worried about her well-being. But I'm positive that her emotional state was being adversely affected by something very real that had happened, not that the state of mind came first and created something terrible but imagined. I hope that helps, because it's the most I can tell you.'

'I'm really going to need to talk to Margo in any case,' Frank said, standing up. 'From what you tell me, she concluded that her husband meant her harm but there was nothing clear-cut or specific, no hard evidence to that effect?'

Monica stood up, shaking her head. 'Not that I know of. You are really going to need to talk to her. I'll let you know the moment I hear from her. I've been trying to get her to talk to the police for some time now.'

As Frank headed for the door, Monica added a final thought. 'I do hope that when you do talk with her, you give some credence to her concerns. She's not crazy. And I really don't trust Max.'

2

In the spare time he could muster, Frank was somewhat of a fan of mysteries. He watched a few cop shows on television and liked a well-done murder mystery novel or movie. As he sat at his desk and computer, plowing through files and paperwork, typing up reports and making e-mail enquiries, he reflected that in the fictional procedurals, it always seemed as if the cops only had one case at a time to which they could devote their total, undivided attention. That was hardly the true state of affairs for a real cop like himself, he thought. It had been a day and a half and he really had not had time to follow up on the strange but unpromising Hesterberg case.

Yesterday Marlon had stopped by his desk to ask how the death threat thing had gone and Frank had been noncommittal, saying only he would need more information. That seemed to have gratified Marlon:

he had gauged the whole thing correctly as a waste of time. Better Frank's than his.

When he found an opportune pause, it occurred to Frank to check back in with Monica Wersching. He punched her number into his aging flip-style mobile phone. She answered after one ring and he identified himself.

'Yes, Detective, I can see on my phone that this call is from you. Phones do that now.'

Frank let that slide. He already knew he was a dinosaur. 'Just wanted to see if you've been able to get in touch with Margo.'

'Curiously, no, I haven't. Her phone goes right to voice mail every time, day or night. I went over and knocked on her door a few times. I even pulled myself up on her back wall and peered over to see if she was in her garden. No sign of her. In fact I was going to go over and ask her super to let me into the apartment today, just to check.'

'Is there someplace she might have gone, taking a vacation or just a respite?

Does she ever do that?'

'Rarely. And if she did, she wouldn't go alone. She would have asked me to come along. Certainly at least she'd have told me.'

'Does Margo have any friends that she might have gone off with?'

'She has friends but nobody she's kept in touch with recently. Excepting for me, that is. She's kept her own counsel largely in the past two years or so.'

There was nothing Frank could really do to pursue the enquiry until he had been able to speak with Margo, so he felt himself at a standstill. For some reason Margo had decided to clear out for the moment. Somehow Frank didn't think any foul play was involved. At worst she was confused and disoriented and might have wandered off and gotten lost.

'That might be a good idea, Ms. Wersching, to go over and check her apartment again. Please let me know if you're unable to locate her. Maybe it'll be advisable to file a missing persons report.'

'Maybe Max got to her, is that what you're thinking?'

Frank hoped she couldn't hear him catching his breath through the phone. 'No, no. Not necessarily. But I might be a little concerned that since she was so worried, she would become distracted and find herself in unfamiliar territory.'

'My sister is not crazy or senile or incompetent, Detective,' Monica replied tartly.

'My apologies; that wasn't what I meant to suggest. Please, just let me know after you've been over to her apartment, OK?'

Monica agreed and ended the conversation. Frank regarded the pile of forms in front of him and dove in once again.

★ ★ ★

It was late in the day when Frank was summoned into the office of his immediate supervisor, Lieutenant Hank Castillo, and handed a phone slip.

'I believe you've already been dealing with this individual,' was all Castillo said, as if that were all that needed to be said by way of explanation. Frank looked down at the slip and swore softly under his breath.

'Think you need to get over there, Frank.'

★ ★ ★

The body still lay in the entrance hallway where it had fallen. There were personnel from the medical examiner's office and the scientific investigation lab bustling around at work, moving economically, skilfully avoiding one another in the tight surroundings. Frank held up the badge he wore on a lanyard for the benefit of the assistant coroner crouching over the corpse. He looked up. 'So what have we got here?'

'Hello, Detective. It seems that he answered his door and whoever was there shot him with a Taser gun. Knocked him down, and apparently killed him. A bit unusual — usually Tasers aren't fatal — but it's not exactly unheard of.' He pointed down to the victim's chest. His shirt had been unbuttoned; there were two sets of nasty dark burns in his pectorals. 'Conceivably cardiac arrest. More will be revealed. His name is — '

'Yes, I know,' interrupted Frank. 'Maurice Hesterberg. I'm familiar with him.'

He pulled aside one of the uniformed officers on the scene and asked to be brought up to speed. Pending confirmation by autopsy and lab work, it was fairly easy to reconstruct what had probably happened to begin with. Hesterberg had answered the doorbell in his condo, where someone had fired into him the two dart-like electrodes of an electroshock weapon, probably a Taser gun. The reconstruction after that became more speculative.

'How long ago?' Frank asked.

'Likely midday, early afternoon.'

'How was he found?'

'The door was left partly open when the attacker fled. It would seem they never entered further into the apartment, just turned and left. Victim's foot partly blocked the door from closing. A neighbor coming down the hall a while later noticed the door ajar and looked in.'

Frank jotted notes. 'I'll need to talk to that neighbor. Anybody else been in here or seen anything? Neighbors, friends?'

The officer shook his head. 'But there was a note.'

'A note?'

One of the lab techs on the floor picked up a clear plastic bag between thumb and forefinger of her gloved hand and passed it up to Frank. 'It was on his chest,' said the assistant coroner. 'We have photos.'

Frank had already pulled on a pair of disposable gloves that he carried with him as a matter of course and he took the bag. There was a regular letter-size piece of paper that had apparently been run through a desktop printer, then folded in half. It bore, in large bold type, three simple words:

IT'S HER FAULT

Frank's brain began to process everything and formulate his plan of action. One thing he knew he had to do as soon as possible was to locate Margo Hesterberg. He stepped out of the hallway, found Monica Wersching's number on his phone, and punched the connect to it. He got her voice mail.

'Monica, this is Detective Frank Vandegraf. I need to know if you've found your sister, and in any case, I need to speak with you. Please get back to me as soon as you get this. I don't care how late it is.'

He turned back to the uniform and asked a few more questions, ascertaining all the details that were available. It appeared that Hesterberg had been home alone; nobody else had apparently even been home on the rest of the floor. 'Where's the neighbor?'

'Two doors down, 1207,' replied the officer. He pointed to his left, facing the door. 'Name's . . . ' He squinted at his own notebook. 'Her . . . herm . . . ?'

Frank looked down at the pad and tried to decipher the scribbles. 'Hermione, looks like.'

'That's it. Hermione Morris.'

Frank thanked the officer and stepped out into the hall and turned left. By now a few neighbors had returned home and were furtively peeking out of their doors at the commotion. Some of the doors closed quickly as Frank strode purposefully down the hall. He knocked on 1207.

The door was answered by a bright-eyed lady who identified herself as Hermione Morris and invited Frank in, once he had shown his ID. She looked as if she were still shaken up by her discovery of Doctor Hesterberg's body.

'So tell me exactly what happened,' Frank began. He had not been asked if he wanted to sit, and to be honest, he didn't.

'Well, I was coming home from work. I'm a book-keeper and I got off early. I was coming down the hallway from the elevator and I happened to notice that Maurice — I mean Professor Hesterberg's — door was slightly ajar. I often say hello to him when we run into one another, so I just sort of called out as I went by. Of course there was no answer. Then I saw the foot in the doorway. I stopped and peeked in and . . . that's when I saw there was a body.'

'Did you open the door?'

She nodded her head up and down vigorously, as if to shake the memory out of her mind. 'Yes, I'm afraid I did. I saw him lying there.'

'What did you do next?'

'I turned and ran for my apartment. I panicked. It was horrible. It didn't even occur to me he might not be dead. He looked dead.'

'Do you remember hearing or seeing anything else? Any indication there might have been someone else in the apartment?'

'I don't remember anything. As I said, I was shocked. All that occurred to me was to run, to get safe in my own place.'

'And you called the police immediately?'

'Well . . . I probably took a few minutes to calm myself down.'

Frank had already noticed a bit of the aroma of gin on Hermione's breath. 'Maybe you took a few deep breaths, had a drink to relax yourself, things like that?'

'Yes, that's exactly what I did, in fact. After a few short minutes I was in possession of my faculties again, and I telephoned the police. It couldn't have been more than five minutes or so.'

Frank's ever-present notebook was open and he was jotting rapidly as he spoke. 'Did you leave your apartment again after that at all, perhaps to take another look, find someone else to tell about it, anything like that?'

'No, I've been in here ever since. To tell you the truth, I'm still spooked about going out in that hall again.'

'Did you perhaps call another neighbor, the building manager or superintendent?'

'There is no building superintendent. There are maintenance people that come during the day, but try to find one. Everybody on our floor works and wouldn't be home yet — everyone but Professor Hesterberg, that is. He's often home during the week. Oh dear. I mean, he *was* often home. This is so awful.'

'Perhaps you called a friend to decompress, tell them what happened?'

'Yes, in fact. I called my friends Renée and Simon. I talked about it with Renée for a while and she helped me calm down. She said I had done exactly the right thing and should just stay in here tonight, have a drink and read or watch television, and that's what I plan to do.'

'And you didn't see or hear anything else that comes to mind, anything at all?'

She thought for a long time before shaking her head. 'No, I can't recall a thing, Detective.'

'All right, thank you, Miss? Mrs.?'

'It's Miss, I suppose. Divorced, though I decided to keep his last name. Didn't get much else of his to keep when all was said and done. Most people call me Hermione. Feel free to call me Hermione if you're comfortable.' She gave him a bit of a mischievous smile. Marlon might have liked her, Frank reflected.

'Thank you, Miss Morris. Here's my card in case you think of anything else that might be of help. I think your plan to stay in tonight is a good one.'

He scanned the room quickly and his eyes lit on a table by the couch that faced a wide-screen television. The blue-cast gin bottle was resting on the table next to a glass and a silver bucket of ice. It was hard to tell how far down the level, but he figured Hermione was set for the evening. He wondered if she'd be watching

Gaslight on the classic movie channel.

He returned to the crime scene and carefully walked around, staying out of the way of the techs at work but trying to absorb whatever information he could. He compared his memories of being here two days previously, replayed his conversation with Hesterberg and looked around for something — anything — that might afford an insight. Had anything been moved? Was anything clearly disturbed?

He asked the techs a few questions. It appeared from the evidence that the assailant had not entered further into the room, and had touched very little, if anything. They were dusting for prints on the doorbell and the door. It was conceivable the attacker had avoided touching much of anything. Had he (or she) rung the bell, or knocked? There was a peephole in the door. Logic dictated Hesterberg wouldn't have just opened the door to anybody; it likely was someone he recognized and knew. Maybe even was expecting.

Frank looked around for the phone. It was resting on the kitchen counter. Was there a pad? Perhaps he had written something down? No, nothing to be found. No notes, not even on the refrigerator. Nothing written anywhere.

Just that crazy note. IT'S HER FAULT.

What did that mean? Was it Margo?

Well, if Hesterberg had been surprised at the door by his wife and she had killed him right there and then, he wouldn't exactly have had time to sit down at his computer and print out a note like that and bring it back with him.

He asked the techs if someone could find and inspect Hesterberg's computer and printer, see if there was any record of having created a word-processed file or printed it, and fingerprint the keyboard. There was a study/den where Hesterberg worked, and they located the electronics there, along with another phone (no notepads there either) and went to work on them.

It was a long shot, but he was grasping at straws here. Likely the assailant had not entered the room, so they would not have gone to the computer and printed out the note. Either he or she had brought it with them with the specific idea of leaving it behind, or Hesterberg already had created it and had it in his possession at the moment he opened the door and was killed.

Frank walked around further, slowly checking every room. Was anything standing out to him?

His phone buzzed. It was Monica. He snapped it open.

'Detective? You called me?'

'Did you locate Margo? Was she in her apartment?'

'No. I went over there tonight; the super went in with me. We looked all over. No sign of her.'

'Did it look as if she had packed or taken anything?'

'I didn't really look. Why?'

'Is there anywhere you can think of that she might go? I need to locate her as soon as I can.'

'Has something happened?'

'I can't talk about that right this moment. What I need to know is, is there some way I can find Margo?'

'I can't think of anything.'

'Can you do me a favor and call her super back; tell her I'm coming over and will need to get into her apartment? Just to let her know; it'll save a few minutes. Tell her not to go into the apartment herself, just to expect me shortly.'

'Well, sure. But what's going on? Is Max making more threats?'

'As I said, I can't tell you anything just yet. Thanks for helping me out.' He snapped the phone shut and took one last look around the scene. There was nothing else he could think of just yet.

The apartment would be sealed off for at least a few days. He could come back fresh tomorrow when he might have more concrete evidence to work with. He headed out to the elevator. The techs had already fingerprinted it and no doubt had done some fingerprinting in the lobby, but he knew those were long shots. How many people passed through that lobby and this elevator every day? Still, he admired the thoroughness of the department's crew.

* * *

Judy, the Super Lady, was waiting to buzz him in as soon as he hit the front door. He didn't even have to come down the stairs; she was in the lobby, looking apprehensive, by the time he had come through both sets of glass entry doors.

'What's up, Detective?' she asked.

'If you can let me in to Margo Hesterberg's apartment it would be greatly appreciated,' he said brusquely.

'Glad to see you too. Sure, follow me.' She turned around and headed back down the hall to the rear of the building, twirling the key on her ring in one hand as she walked.

Frank wasn't quite sure what he expected to find, but he knew the first thing he wanted to look for. It was a small apartment; finding the bedroom was not a challenge. He donned a new pair of disposable gloves and opened the closet door. The tiny closet smelled of some kind of sachet. There were a few empty hangers on the rod.

He turned to the bureau and pulled open the top drawer, which held underwear, socks, and other small items. There were spaces. The second drawer was mostly shirts, and again he saw uneven piles.

'Would you say Margo Hesterberg is a careful woman?' he asked as he perused the contents of the drawers in rapid order.

'Um, what exactly do you mean?'

'Would you say she's a *neat* woman? This apartment looks very well kept, everything in its place. No clutter.'

'Don't know her all that well, but yeah, I'd say she's a bit *fastidious*,' Judy replied, punching the word sarcastically. 'Not that I come in here all that often, but let me tell you, if this were my place and my hubby weren't around, I'd probably have a bit more of a mess, you know?'

'Not the kind of person who'd make uneven piles in her drawers like these,' Frank said, more to himself than to her. 'She's packed recently.'

He looked around the closet again. There was a shelf above the clothes rod, with a few boxes stored away. There was an open space at the top. Maybe that was how Margo had arranged it, but Frank's hunch was that there had been a suitcase of some kind up there.

'When was the last time you saw Margo Hesterberg?' he asked.

She thought for a moment. 'Let me see . . . a few days ago? Yeah, ran into her coming off the elevator the other day.'

'She was coming off the elevator? She lives on the ground floor!'

'No, no, I was coming off the elevator. Coming down from a tenant upstairs. She was in the basement near my apartment, in the laundry.'

'She was doing her laundry? What day was that?'

Judy's lips moved as she thought hard about it, counting. 'Four days ago. No, five. It was Saturday. Five days ago.'

'Did you talk about anything? Did she say anything about planning to do anything or go anywhere?'

Judy shrugged. 'Naw, nothing like that. We just said hi, ships passing in the night. I'm not that involved or friendly with any of my tenants.'

'She had laundry with her?'

'I'm not sure, but she was coming out

of the laundry room. That's the last time I saw her.'

'Your husband is superintendent with you too, right? Would he possibly have encountered her at some later time?'

'Well, let's go ask him,' Judy said. 'When you're done here.'

'Could you maybe call him and ask him to come up here?'

Judy sighed. 'Yeah, sure. I'll go get him. You seem trustworthy enough up here.'

'Actually I'd prefer you stay; can you call him?' Frank knew protocol well enough to play it safe. He was already on shaky ground, having gained entry to this apartment without a warrant or due cause. Likely whatever he might uncover here was useless as evidence in a court of law if it ever came to that.

But he had no idea where this line of enquiry was heading — accusations of falsifying or contaminating evidence would be another matter altogether. If they later found it necessary to return with a bona fide warrant, he wanted to do his best to sidestep questions about things like planted evidence, so he needed to *not* be left alone here for even a moment. He was fortunate she was being so obliging in any case, but then she still was laboring under the misapprehension that he was here because Margo might be in danger.

She gave off another almighty sigh, rolled her eyes skyward, and pulled her phone from her pocket.

Frank continued to move about the apartment, looking for any other signs that might tell him where Margo could have gone. Again he checked for pads by the phone, without luck. He looked for a computer and found an aging one on a stand in her bedroom, but he couldn't do much more than power it up. He couldn't access anything without a password.

Judy's husband, a burly balding man in a white T-shirt who introduced himself as Steve, arrived in the apartment. Frank asked a few quick questions and established that Steve had not encountered 'Miz Hesterberg' any time since his wife had. He left another card with them both and asked that they contact him if they remembered or learned anything that might help him locate her.

It was getting late but Frank needed to put things together while the trail might still be warm. Heading back to his car, he struggled to find some sense in what had happened.

Max Hesterberg insists Margo is trying to kill him, but has nothing definite to back it up, just 'feelings.'

Margo, who has made similar claims to her sister that Hesterberg threatened *her*, disappears.

Hesterberg turns up dead.

Margo apparently has moved out, to parts unknown, with whatever a suitcase will hold. She likely hasn't gone far.

Frank pulled out his phone to call Monica. He apologized for bothering her again but said he needed to speak with her one more time. Yes, right now.

* * *

'So you're telling me Max is dead?' Monica was having a hard time making sense of it all. They were once again sitting in her parlor. Frank was once again jotting in his notebook. 'Murdered? You

47

think Margo murdered him?'

'I don't know who murdered him, but yes, he was killed today. Your sister is certainly a suspect. Once again I have to ask you to think carefully. Is there anywhere Margo might have gone, anything you can tell me that might help me find her?'

Monica's eyes were wide and looked glazed. She just kept shaking her head. 'She couldn't have done this. It makes no sense.'

Frank repeated his question. This time she seemed to snap back to reality and she looked at him, continuing to shake her head. 'No, I've got no idea where she could be. She didn't do this, Detective.'

'All the more reason why I need to find her right away. If she's innocent, she needs to convince me of that, make me see it.'

He was getting nowhere. He stood up and packed away his notebook. 'You've got my card. Please, call me any time night or day if you come up with anything, if you hear from her, anything that would help. If she's innocent I can help her, but I've got to find her, do you understand?'

Monica also rose, nodding her head gravely.

'One last thing: do you have a recent photo of her that I can borrow?' He realized he had never seen Margo Hesterberg.

'Yes, of course.' Frank expected her to run for a photo album or a framed picture on a wall or a mantle. Instead she reached for a cell phone on a nearby table and began pressing buttons. She held up her phone to show a picture of her and her sister smiling at an outdoor café. Margo looked very much like her sister, only a bit more youthful, her hair and face a little fuller, with a more animated and buoyant expression.

No more framed snapshots. Frank again felt like a dinosaur as he looked at the phone screen. 'Can you email that to me?' he sighed. He reached back into his pocket for his pencil so he could write his address for her.

'Certainly. But why write it? Don't you have it on your phone so you can just send it to me?'

'No, Ms. Wersching, I'm afraid my

phone doesn't do that. But my email address is easy enough.' He looked about for something on which to write. Monica smiled in spite of her state of mind.

'Just tell it to me,' she said. 'I'll send you a picture right now.' She hit more buttons as he rattled it off and then pressed SEND. There was a 'bwwwoop' sound and she said, 'Done.'

Oh brave new world, thought Frank. He figured Dr. Max would have approved that he knew the line. He might have said, 'So you're a reader, then . . . '

★ ★ ★

Frank stopped back at the station before calling it a night. The night shift had taken over and it was fairly quiet, which he welcomed. He sat at his desk, flipping through his notes, trying to organize everything and find a pattern. He reconstructed Hesterberg's condo in his mind's eye, the crime scene . . . then Margo's apartment, looking for something to jump out and announce itself. Years of experience had taught him that this was often fruitful. But there was nothing. Nothing yet.

The photo of Margo, he discovered, was indeed waiting for him on his computer. He clicked the onscreen button to print out several copies. As he waited for the printer, he started scribbling his course of action onto a legal pad with a ballpoint pen.

First order of business: find Margo Hesterberg. Underlined twice.

Second order of business: find out anybody else who might fit the role as the murderer. That is to say, being known to Hesterberg sufficiently for him to open the door to them while also having motive to harm him.

Next destination, check the university.

He jotted a few more thoughts down, then walked over to the shared printer and picked up the copies of Margo's picture.

One last thing he could do tonight, for what it was worth. He returned to his computer and sent out emails in his established routes throughout the department, with attached photo, requesting an alert on Margo Hesterberg. In the morning he could follow up on that with more alerts and requests for BOLOs — 'be on the lookout' notices — through various channels.

He yawned. Nothing else he could do tonight unless Monica called. Something else experience had taught him was that even while he slept, his mind would keep working, looking for connections. There had been times when he had awakened in the morning with an insight bouncing around his head that hadn't been in there the night before. Might as well call it a night.

3

The night had not provided new insight, Frank had to admit. But then again it hadn't provided much sleep, either. He had found himself awake several times, his brain racing in overdrive. He was awake when his alarm went off. He wondered if guilt wasn't a component of that. Could he have taken more seriously the concerns of Maurice Hesterberg and perhaps prevented his killing?

Second guessing came with the job, he knew by now, and it was best to try to put those kinds of thoughts out of mind as best he could. Get the feet on the ground before the head can completely kick in. Shave, shower, coffee, breakfast, get in the car, drive to work, all by the numbers. Do not listen to the head until absolutely necessary.

His yellow legal pad with his notes of the evening before was still on his desk to greet him when he arrived at the squad room. Things were already bustling around him — detectives and officers scurrying about and talking loudly, everybody multi-tasking to try to get that much more done.

The city was always generously dropping something new on the detectives' door-step, and it was always a challenge to stay on top of it all. He loved the oddness of the name of his unit: Personal Crimes. Some years back it had been called Special Crimes, and before that plain old Robbery-Homicide, but at some point a commission decided Personal Crimes had a more meaningful ring to it, the sound of a true mission statement.

They still dealt with basically the same types of felony offenses: murders, severe assaults, serious robberies. The unit that handled burglaries and similar non-violent crimes had been renamed Property Crimes, which to his thinking was somewhat more lackluster. Frank had to wonder who would ever want to transfer to something called Property Crimes.

He turned on his computer, gave his prior night's notes a once-over, and began to map out his day. Getting out an official

BOLO on Margo was his priority, along with whatever else he could do to get the word out on her. Next he would head to the university to try to find close associates of Hesterberg.

His thoughts were interrupted by the buzzy ringtone of his cell phone. He fished it out of his pocket. 'Vandegraf.'

'Yeah, Frank, this is Coulton, up here in Sunnyview. I got your email alert this morning first thing.'

Sunnyview was the northernmost district of the city, and formed part of the boundary with its neighbor city. It was mostly suburban, with malls, restaurants, hotels, and the like.

Sam Coulton was a detective and worked the northern division. He was a righteous cop in Frank's eyes, unsentimental to the point of cynicism and not exactly lovable, but righteous nonetheless. Frank always included him in his notices and enquiries and had often been rewarded for doing so.

'Yeah, Sam, what's up?'

'I've found your girl.'

'My girl? Margo Hesterberg?'

'The same.'

'Where are you?' Frank realized he had begun to rise out of his seat. He sat back down, grabbed his pen and pulled his pad over to jot down the address.

'I'm at the Pleasant Dreams Inn, the one up near the Expressway. You know it?' Pleasant Dreams was a regional chain, on the inexpensive side of things but famously clean and family friendly.

'Oh yeah. Where exactly?'

'Room 816. All the way in the back, past the pool.'

'Don't know how you found her, but this is great. Hang on to her, I'll be right over.'

'Well, that's the thing,' sighed Sam. 'She's not going anywhere. You can take your time.'

★ ★ ★

There were several city vans in the parking lot, belonging to the coroner and the Scientific Investigation Division. Frank worked his way through the uniformed officers who were doing their best to wrangle the herd of curious and excited people who had gathered just outside of the building.

He attached his badge to his lanyard and hung it around his neck to facilitate the task of continually showing it to still another beleaguered uniform. Inside, the hallway itself was fairly clear until he reached the room, where the usual clump of techs and medical examiners were at work.

Sam himself was standing in the room, hands in pockets, talking with a tech. They were next to a queen-size bed upon which lay a body that had been covered with a sheet for the moment. Sam saw Frank and nodded in acknowledgment, then motioned him over. He lifted the sheet off the head of the body.

It was indeed Margo Hesterberg, or at least she was a dead ringer for her picture. She was on her back, arms at her sides, eyes starkly open and staring at the ceiling. Frank could see the ligature marks on her bare throat.

'This your girl?' Sam asked brightly.

'Sure looks like her,' Frank said, rubbing the back of his neck.

'You still do that,' Sam remarked, pointing to Frank's hand on his neck. What, now he was famous for it? Self-consciously, he dropped his hand to his side.

'There was ID?' Frank asked.

'Yeah, her bag was on that chair over there. Margo Hesterberg she is.'

'What happened?'

'Housekeeper found her this morning. Funny thing — you know those signs you can put on your door, one side says DO NOT DISTURB and the other says MAID SERVICE REQUESTED? Well, the sign requesting service was on the doorknob, so she unlocked the door and came in. There she was.'

'What time was this?' Frank asked, starting to look about the room.

'Early, maybe seven thirty. Best guess is she was murdered yesterday, maybe last night. We got here right about the time I called you this morning. I was first up and got the call.'

'Has she been touched or processed in any way?'

'Not yet. When you said you were on the way over, and the MEs showed up, I told 'em to wait for you.'

Sam pointed alongside Margo's body on the still-made bed. 'Looks like she's been strangled. That the murder weapon, you think?' A long beige fabric cord, something like one would use to pull open curtains or drapes, lay next to her.

'If so, they bothered to remove the cord from her throat after she was dead,' Frank observed. 'It's like they took their time.'

'There's also this,' Sam continued, pointing to something peeking out from under the sheet that had been thrown over her. Sam reached out and swiped away the sheet without touching what was beneath. It brought to mind the old magician's trick, swiping a tablecloth out from under a fully set dinner table without disturbing a plate or the candelabra. Frank almost expected him to exclaim, 'Ta-daa!'

There was a piece of light cardboard, perhaps five inches square, lying alongside her body. On it had been printed, with a broad-tip black marker in large block letters, three words:

IT'S HIS FAULT

He had already donned his gloves and now he bent over the body, careful to not come into contact, and gingerly picked up the cardboard by the smallest edge of a corner. He turned it over and looked at it for a long time. There was nothing else written on the card anywhere, no marks or smudges. It was immaculate. Even the printing was neat and precise.

'What in . . . ?' Frank began.

'Pretty cryptic, I'd say,' Sam offered. 'Who's 'he'?'

'You don't know the half of it,' Frank muttered. He replaced the card where he had found it. Now he leaned back over the body carefully in order to inspect it. She was fully clothed in a blue long-sleeved shirt and denim slacks, and still had on short white socks and a pair of tennis shoes. Frank carefully picked up each hand and inspected it. Her fingernails were clipped short. Likely she had struggled — strangulation is a most unpleasant way to die — but the odds were reduced of their getting any skin cells under the nails.

'Looks to me like she was taken by surprise,' Sam observed. 'Not a huge fight out of her.'

Frank inspected the head and face. 'No bruising that I can see. Doesn't look like she was knocked unconscious first or anything.' He motioned to the medical examiner in charge, who came closer. 'You can go ahead,' Frank said. 'Just make sure the techs get pictures first, OK?' The ME nodded wearily. Apparently he was at the end of his shift rather than the beginning. He wagged a finger at a couple of the techs and passed the word.

The moment they approached, Frank pointed out the card and made sure they knew to photograph it profusely, print it, and bag it for further processing as evidence. He also made sure they photographed and bagged the cord.

Frank watched as they turned the body over and began a thorough examination. Of course there would be a much more thorough one once the body had been transferred to the coroner's office, but whatever he could glean right now would possibly be of great importance.

'Time of death?' he asked at one point. The examiner gave him a frame of sometime between five and eight the previous night.

Margo was still alive when Max had been killed. But with all due respect to the dead, she hadn't been cleared yet.

Officers had canvassed the floor and nobody in any of the nearby rooms could remember having heard any noises of an argument, a struggle, an assault. The manager had pointed out that at midweek occupancy was lower, and those who were here were possibly out to dinner or elsewhere.

Frank's own inspection of the motel room didn't yield any insights. There were no obvious signs of forced entry into the room or any kind of violent struggle or confrontation. The assailant had apparently gained entry without much problem, had surprised Margo and overcome her easily. Had she simply let him or her into the room?

Her handbag yielded nothing unusual. There was a wallet, keys, the other typical things one would expect. Frank found nothing particularly worthy of attention. It would all be collected and recorded and he could look through it later. He did take the car keys, making sure to inform the techs that he would be returning them shortly.

Margo's small suitcase — more an overnight bag really — sat closed on the usual luggage stand found in these kinds of rooms. She hadn't bothered to put anything in any of the drawers. A blouse and a jacket looked lonely hanging in the otherwise empty closet. Her hotel key card sat on the nightstand next to the bed.

According to desk records, she had checked in Tuesday, three days ago, using her real name. She had used a credit card to reserve the room through the coming weekend. Frank made a note to stop by the desk and see who had checked her in.

Sam broke his reverie. 'I assume this one's yours now.' He looked downright relieved. Frank nodded, twisting his mouth into a grimace. He didn't want it, but it had to be his. Among other things, that meant it fell to him to inform

Monica Wersching about her sister's fate. That would have to be his next stop.

He finished his inspection, consulted with the techs, made a few more requests. He knew most of the crew and for the most part knew he could rely on their expertise and thoroughness. Then he headed off to the front desk. The officers outside had dispersed a fair amount of the crowd and he easily traversed the parking lot to the lobby.

He at least lucked out in that the clerk who had checked in Margo was on duty. He was a neat and nervous young man, perhaps in his late twenties, evidently seriously shaken by the death of Margo Hesterberg. He vaguely recalled her arrival and dug out the sign-in record. She was alone. She had left a credit card number as a deposit until check-out, along with her real name and home address and her car's license plate number.

The clerk explained that the hotel required every guest display a parking pass in their car's front window while in the lot, and this was checked regularly. There was a description of Margo's car.

Frank recorded the details in his note-book. The clerk wasn't much help beyond that. His memory corresponded with what the uniforms had learned: she had checked in on Tuesday and booked the room for seven days in total. She had made no small talk that the clerk could remember, and he had not seen her since.

Frank asked for the manager and ascertained that nobody currently on duty had had any contact with Margo in the past two days. The night shift would be coming in in a few hours and the manager would also ask them the same question; Frank was welcome to check back with him again.

Frank wandered out into the parking lot and began looking for Margo's small gold Honda Fit. It wasn't difficult to locate. He tried Margo's key alarm and heard the low beep and click that indicated he had unlocked the door. It was a fastidiously kept car (Judy the super had characterized Margo correctly, it seemed) — clean, free of any loose refuse, and even with a slight scent of floral air freshener. Her parking pass was displayed on the dash in the window.

Only a small square box of tissues rested on the passenger seat. He checked the box and found nothing else stuck into it — just tissues. There was very little in the glove box besides the vehicle registration, nothing in any of the other little nooks and crannies that newer cars seemed to feature. He checked under the seats and opened the hatchback to look into the rear storage area. The car seemed almost empty. If Margo had indeed murdered Max, she hadn't brought the murder weapon here with her.

When he was convinced he wasn't going to find anything, he locked the car and trudged back to Room 816 to return the key and tell the techs where they would find the Honda. There was nothing more he could do here. He would have to wait on the techs for further information. He thanked Sam for getting in touch with him and departed.

His next task was one he did not relish. He pulled out his phone to call Monica Wersching and say he was on his way over.

★ ★ ★

Not surprisingly, Monica did not take the news well but, all things considered, Frank thought she took it better than he had anticipated. She had invited him in with visible apprehension, they had sat down in her parlor, and she had broken into tears before he had even finished his first sentence.

Over the years this unpleasant duty had fallen to Frank way too many times, and it never got any easier or less awkward. He had become inured to gruesome crime scenes and grisly modes of death, but had never hardened to breaking the heart of a loved one. He waited it out in respectful silence.

She regained her composure after a few minutes, wiped her eyes, and steadied her voice to ask him for further details of Margo's death. He kept it as simple as he could.

One of her first comments was, 'So there's no possible way that Max killed her.'

'No, her death definitely occurred after his. I'm sorry, I know this is hard, but can you think of anyone else who might have had reason to do this?'

'My God, no.' She shook her head repeatedly, staring down at her hands. 'Margo was a sweetheart.'

'Let's go back to those break-ins Margo believed were occurring in her apartment. Could that have been done by someone other than Max?'

'I don't know who.'

'Was there anybody who had a key to her place?'

'I didn't even have one, and I was the closest person to her.'

'If she were to go away, did she ever have, I don't know, plants needing watering? A cat or some pet needing to be fed?'

'No pets. Margo might have had plants but she never went away so she never asked me to come water them. It's possible lately she was so agitated that I think she just got rid of them or let them die.'

'So there's nobody she might have asked to look in on her place at any point?'

'The only people who might have had a key to her place were the supers. The property managers.' She thought for a minute and then hastily added, 'I can't believe they would have done anything to hurt her.'

'And there's nobody you can think of that she'd been in touch with recently, nobody you saw her with, nobody she might have mentioned?'

Monica gave that some thought. It was clear she was having trouble concentrating at the moment. 'No. I can't think of anyone she had been in touch with besides Max. As I told you before, she kept her own counsel in recent times.'

Frank tried a few more questions but nothing seemed promising. From experience he realized there was only so far he could go at this point, so he thanked Monica and said he would be in touch and asked her to call with anything she might think would be helpful.

'I suppose I'll need to go organize Margo's things,' Monica said rather distractedly as Frank rose from his seat.

'Maybe it would be better to wait on that,' Frank said. 'Let me talk to the supers first. Give it a couple of days, OK?' Monica just nodded. Thinking on his last trip to the apartment, somehow he didn't think it would yield anything useful, but what else was there?

At the building entry, he rang the intercom for Steve and Judy's apartment but didn't have to wait to be buzzed in, because a young man pulled the door open and slipped by him, followed by Judy herself.

'Detective,' she greeted him dryly. 'We must stop meeting like this. My husband is starting to get suspicious.'

'I'm afraid I'm going to need to get into Margo Hesterberg's apartment again.'

She rolled her eyes. 'I don't think she's come back, and I'm guessing you haven't found her yet, huh?'

'Actually, I have, but let me tell you inside.'

Now she looked alarmed. 'Something happen to her?'

'Just let me in, OK?'

Judy yelled out to the young man, who had stopped and turned to wait for her. 'Emil, I'll be along in a few minutes. You know what to do with the trash, right?' He nodded and resumed walking out to the street.

'Pickup day tomorrow morning, we

have to roll the garbage bins out to the street for the trucks. Come on, I'll get the key.' He followed her to the elevator.

'Your son?' asked Frank.

'Emil? Oh, no. We've got a grown son but he lives in another state. Emil just does work for us, like when we need a strong back or an extra pair of hands. Good guy.'

A quick stop at her apartment to get a key and back upstairs, and they were at the door. Frank stopped her before they entered. She looked at him apprehensively. 'Is she all right?'

'No, I'm afraid not. Judy, Margo Hesterberg is dead. We found her body this morning.'

That stopped her cold in her tracks. She just stared at Frank for a moment, her mouth agape. 'Wh-what happened?' she stammered.

'She was murdered.' Frank's long silence finally got through to her that he was not going to be very forthcoming about details. She fumbled the key into the lock and opened the door. Frank had already pulled out a pair of his disposable gloves and was donning them.

'I'm going to have to ask you to not touch anything this time.' He stepped into the apartment, looking around.

'I've been in here now and then,' Judy said, 'including with you. I've touched plenty. My prints are all around.'

'I'm not worried about your prints so much as I am of something more recent being covered up,' Frank said. 'I understand someone had been breaking into this apartment and moving things around. Did Margo ever mention that to you?'

'Uh, yeah, sure. She wanted the locks changed. We did that for her about two weeks ago.'

'What exactly did she tell you had been happening?'

'She said she came home one evening to find a vase broken, just smashed to pieces on her hall floor. She told me it had been in another room.'

'And there was no cat or dog to knock it over, right?'

'No, Margo has no pets. I mean, *had* no pets. We discourage them. Anyway, she claimed the vase had to have been carried

72

from the other room and brought into the hallway. She said a few other things had happened . . . she called them 'subtle' things. Items moved from one place to another.'

'Did she specify any of those?'

Judy thought about it, hands on hips. 'I kind of didn't pay a lot of attention. Steve thinks she's a little ditsy and she was being paranoid. He thinks she just forgot she had moved the . . . yes that was one! She said a group of old photos had been taken out of her dresser drawer and spread out on her bed one night!' She paused to think some more. 'There was something about something from college. A transcript, I think she might have said, a yearbook, something like that, that were stored in her closet, and she found them on her night table. I don't remember much more than that.'

'That was pretty good, actually.'

'Well, Steve made a kind of joke about it, saying she was reliving her past, pulling out old memories, and then just forgot. That's why it might have stuck in my mind.'

Frank was carefully looking around the entry hall, bending down to check the carpet and floor, inspecting the small photographs on the wall, slowly working his way to the living room. Even with his gloves he was trying to touch as little as possible. Very possibly he might have the techs in here as soon as he could. 'From just where was Margo returning when she would find these things? I understand she didn't go out much.'

'Pretty much always from visiting her sister, I think. She and I weren't exactly friendly, you know? We don't get real friendly with the tenants; it can cause complications. But the impression I got was that she stayed home a lot, kept to herself.'

'And how did you get that impression, exactly?'

Super Judy might have been getting a bit unnerved by Frank, as he asked questions while seemingly paying all his attention to the apartment. She shifted the weight back and forth on her feet.

'Well, I never saw any visitors, except her sister . . . seldom ran into her around the building, Steve once or twice remarked the same thing. We do keep our eyes open for strangers around here.'

Somehow Frank suspected that Steve and Judy knew considerably more about some of their tenants than they would have let on. He had known a few nosy, gossipy property managers in his day. What had tipped her off, she seemed to be saying, was that she did *not* know anything about anyone visiting Margo.

He was in the living room now, beginning to methodically make his way around the room. He raised a hand to Judy. 'Please, I'd appreciate it if you stayed in the hall for now. Who has a key to this apartment?'

'What exactly do you mean?'

'Well, of course Margo had one. More than one?'

'She got one set from us, for the front door, the apartment, and the outdoor garbage bin area. Naturally she could have duplicated them, tenants usually do, but we gave her one set.'

'And of course you have a key to this apartment.'

Judy raised her hands as if to say, 'Well,

here we are, aren't we?' and remained silent, giving Frank a wide-eyed look.

'Anybody else to your knowledge?'

'Not that I know of. If the management company or anybody like that visits, they have to come to us.'

Frank nodded, bending over to look under an old low sofa. 'And you and Steve keep a close watch on your sets of keys, I'm sure.'

'We certainly do. You saw — they're kept in a closet, and we lock it if we're not going to be around for any reason.'

He reached under the sofa and gingerly picked something up between thumb and forefinger. He brought it out and looked at it closely. It seemed to be a little shard of glass or ceramic.

'Do you know what the vase that was broken looked like?'

'Search me. She swept it up and threw it away. Nobody ever came in here to clean.'

Frank put the little shard back where he had found it. 'She kept this place pretty clean by herself. No housekeeper or maid or anything, then?'

'Not that I know of. And I usually see them when they come in here. As I said, we're on the lookout for unfamiliar types in the building. We ask tenants to inform us if they are going to have regular visitors of that type. You know, so when we see them we know they're supposed to be here, they're not suspicious.'

Frank had resumed his slow steady perusal of the room. 'Seen anybody like that around here in the past few weeks?'

'Suspicious sorts?' Again she paused to consider. 'No, not really. Nobody.'

'What does 'not really' mean, exactly?'

'Well, sure there have been people coming and going in the building all the time. But nobody we couldn't *account* for, you know? Delivery people, plumber, legitimate visitors, that kind of stuff.'

'You'd know if someone was 'not accounted for,' then?'

'We keep an eye out, yes.'

'And nobody like that came to Margo's door to your knowledge? Package delivery, repairman, anything like that?'

'Repair and maintenance, we have to call for; and no, nobody like that. No deliveries that I know of. People have to ring to get in and that generally means I'm aware of them.'

Frank continued through the apartment, asking Judy to remain in the hallway until he arrived in the bedroom.

'Do you happen to know where she found the photographs or the yearbook or whatever it was? Or where they came from?' he called out.

'I never saw any of it,' she called back. 'She said the stuff came from her dresser and her closet, so I guess it was all in there. She said some of it was laid out across her bed and some of it across her living room table.'

He carefully pulled down each of the cardboard boxes he had seen earlier in the closet and checked them. One did indeed hold a pile of college memorabilia: yearbooks, a diploma, various records such as transcripts, even a few old essays and papers. At the very top of one box was a typical college term paper with a cover page bearing her name, with a note scrawled in red across the top. Frank labored his way through the writing:

'Nicely done, very nicely done, but then I shall always expect nice things from you. Max.' The date was twenty-six years ago.

Max had begun to court his student, and it seemed he wasn't very discreet about it either.

A pile of photos filled another box. They weren't stacked as neatly as most of her other things. Possibly, he surmised, these were the pictures she found spread out across her bed, and she had hurriedly repacked them and stuffed them up into the closet. They were photos from her school days or thereabouts. Most of them featured a girl who looked a lot like the picture he had of Margo, only younger and more jubilant. He didn't recognize anybody else in the pictures except for Max — a younger thinner Max with more hair, including youthful sideburns and a goatee. He returned the photos to the box and left it alongside the others out on the floor.

He proceeded in similar fashion for another half hour, then paused and called the station and asked to be put through to the crime scene investigators. He requested a processing team and made special note of the boxes he had laid out in the bedroom. It was all a long shot that any prints or other evidence could be pulled off this material, but he had to give it a shot.

He checked the back door. There were two strong locks on it. No noticeable scratches or marks around the hardware to suggest forced entry. The door had glass panes but they were solid, no digs or gouges.

Finally he returned to the entryway. 'Margo never reported any break-in from the back yard, did she?'

Judy was beginning to look bored. 'Never. But she did have us install that second lock on the door.'

'There will be a crime scene investigation team coming here. I'm going to ask you to stay out of here before they arrive, and to direct them here and let them in, OK?'

'Sure. I'll be happy to stay out. This is starting to give me the creeps already.'

As Judy locked the door behind them, Frank said, 'I have to go to my car to get something. Can you let me back in in just a second?'

He returned with a small roll of yellow police tape reading DO NOT CROSS and a roll of adhesive, and affixed a criss-cross across the front of the jamb that did not touch the door itself. The techs would remove it when they arrived, but hopefully it would keep out anybody else who was curious.

'I told you, I'm not going in there,' Judy said.

'It's not for you,' Frank replied. Neither one totally bought that, he reflected.

'Anyway, I gotta go help Emil move those bins. Until next time, Detective.'

4

It wasn't really that late, it was just feeling that way already. His next stop would be the State University, which seemed the next logical step in trying to track down information about Max Hesterberg. He decided he'd start with the administration offices, out of courtesy, and work his way down to the English Department and some of Max's colleagues.

The first person to meet with him was Dean Marian Wormley, a lean, dignified woman with a well-styled mane of silvery hair. She greeted Frank in the reception area with a look of deep sadness. 'Detective, we've all heard the news about dear Doctor Hesterberg and we are all devastated. What a horrible thing.' She motioned to a large maroon velvet upholstered sofa and they both sat down.

'Yes, ma'am,' Frank replied seriously.

''Dean' is fine,' she corrected. ''Dean Wormley' is my correct title.' She looked at him expectantly.

'Of course, uh, Dean Wormley. It was a terrible tragedy. My condolences to you and everyone at the university.' Titles seemed to be extremely important to academic types, he considered.

'So how may I be of help, Detective?'

'I would like to speak with anyone who knew Doctor Hesterberg well. I have a lot of questions. You're a logical place to begin. Did you know him well?'

'I must admit, I hardly knew the man at all. We spoke at a few gatherings and social events here. He seemed a nice enough man — struck me as quite self-confident, perhaps to the point of being a bit supercilious. Competent enough from what I saw of his faculty records. He published some well-received papers in his area of expertise.'

'Were there ever any disagreements, controversies, involving you?'

She frowned, then raised her eyebrows. 'No. Nothing like that.' She just gazed quietly at him, waiting for his next question. The conversation continued with more abrupt answers and awkward silences. Frank could see it was going nowhere. He thanked her for her time and asked if he might be directed to somebody closer to Hesterberg. She stood up, shook his hand briskly while looking him in the eye, and said, 'Let me know if I might be of any further help to you, Detective Vanderwaal. We all hope you get to the bottom of this.'

'That's Vandegraf,' Frank corrected. 'Thank you, Dean Wormley.'

★ ★ ★

The chairman of the English Department seemed more promising. Mark Wootten said he had known Max Hesterberg for over thirty years and counted him as a valued friend as well as an esteemed colleague. In fact Wootten had counted himself among that suspect cognac-quaffing group known to Margo Hesterberg as Max's 'tavern companions.' It was evident that he was sorely shaken by the death of his friend and wanted to help however he could. Frank remarked that Dean Wormley had recommended he begin his enquiry with Wootten. At the mention of Wormley, Wootten screwed up his face into a sour scowl. 'So you've met the Wicked Witch of the West. Quite a piece of work, that one.'

'She says that she and Hesterberg were not well acquainted.'

'She told you that! Fascinating. Did she mention the knock-down drag-out battles at the budget meetings?'

'Uh, no.'

'Interesting. She must have known it would come out.'

'She and Hesterberg had words?'

'Numerous times. Marian is used to having her way. Max was one to speak his mind. They were the proverbial oil and water. Or perhaps I should say he was gasoline to her bonfire.' Wootten seemed to be searching for additional metaphors so Frank jumped in.

'What did they argue about?'

Wootten waved a hand in dismissal. 'Oh, nothing of import. It was the principle of the thing. Max didn't like her and didn't want her to have her way, so he made himself difficult with her.'

'Did Max make himself difficult with a lot of people?'

'Not really. You have to understand, if Max liked you, he was a big pussy cat. If he took a dislike to you, he would not try to hide it.'

'Let's explore that for a moment, Doc.'

'Mark is fine. You don't need to call me Doc or Doctor.'

Frank raised an eyebrow. Would wonders never cease. 'OK, Mark, what I wonder is, were there many people recently that he might have chosen to be *difficult* with, as you put it?'

Wootten chewed that over for a while before replying. 'No, not really. Max was somewhat quieter than usual of late. I think perhaps he had things on his mind. He was subdued. I know he had some falling out with his wife Margo, and I think it weighed upon him. But my point is, he didn't have his usual verve for confrontation anymore in recent months. I doubt he locked horns with anybody. He seemed happiest to have a brandy with his friends, go for a long walk or work on his current article. Escapism, no doubt.'

'Did he say much about what was

going on with Margo when you got together?'

'Something about her harassing him and accusing him of things of which he said he would be proven innocent.'

'Are you aware that Margo is also dead?'

'The devil you say! No!' Wootten looked genuinely shocked. 'What happened?'

It surprised Frank that news of the crime hadn't spread yet. 'She was also murdered. I believe there's a connection.'

'Murdered, you say! In the same manner as Max? By the same person?'

'I don't know yet. I'm hoping you can help me. I want to come back to things he might have talked about recently, but tell me a little bit about Max and Margo, their history together.'

Frank swore that Wootten's eyes misted as he began to reminisce. 'Those were the days. We were both in the department here. In many ways it was like Never Never Land and we were the Lost Boys. We felt like we were being paid to not grow up. We both absolutely loved literature and could indulge in it around the clock, debating it, discussing it, and of course teaching it to wide-eyed receptive students. Oh, give me some of those today. Now they can't put a decent sentence together, they have no attention spans, no interest, and they expect to get As just for showing up.'

'Um, Doc — I mean, Mark . . . Max and Margo — ?'

'Ah, I digress. Forgive me. Max and I loved our work. We loved it so much that we would take it to the bar and continue to talk about it into the late hours over good whiskey. We wanted to remain eternally youthful and run with the kids.

'Max was a particularly dashing figure: the hair style, the facial hair — even then the faculty gave him grief over that. Trendy clothes designed for people a decade younger. He tried to listen to contemporary music, read contemporary literature as well as his beloved Germans. He was worldly but youthful, brilliant but hip. He liked to hang out with students, often drank with them. I wouldn't be surprised if he smoked pot with them on occasion, but I don't know about that.'

He shrugged. 'His students loved him. Particularly the girls.'

'Margo was his student, as I understand.'

'Oh yes. My, you should have seen her in those days. Full of life. Huge dreamy eyes. She was so taken by Max. He became her faculty advisor for her master's thesis. They started to spend a good deal of time together. Shortly it was a badly kept secret on campus that they were an item.'

'I can't imagine the faculty was pleased about that.'

'Well, no. You have to realize, things were a bit different around here then. People could look the other way. After all, it wasn't like Margo was a child. She was a grad student, probably in her twenties. I don't think that Paula was very happy about it though.'

Frank, who had been jotting in his notebook, stopped and looked up. 'Paula?'

'Oh, you don't know about Paula. Of course not. That's ancient history. The woman with whom he was living. Paula Graham.'

'You're telling me Margo was the other

woman, so to speak?'

'Absolutely. Max fell head over heels for her. She was young and fresh and brilliant. And considerably younger than Paula.'

'Or Max himself,' Frank said, figuring in his head.

'Definitely. Not quite a May — December romance, more perhaps a June — October.' He smirked at his own joke.

'So Paula left and Max and Margo got married.'

'In a nutshell, yes. Leaving out a fair amount of soap-opera grade *sturm und drang*.' More smiles at his own little humor. 'Those were intense years for my friend Max.'

'Very often those kinds of romances don't work out all that well. I mean, where the husband throws over the wife for a younger woman.'

'Yes, we men are great fools in that regard, aren't we? By the way, Max and Paula weren't married. But they had been together for a number of years. In Max's early years here, they were inseparable, for example at social functions and other times when Max wasn't teaching.'

'They grew apart,' Frank suggested. Wootten nodded.

'That had begun to happen before he met Margo. Max and Paula seemed very different. Perhaps that was even why Max turned to Margo.'

'You don't think he just got dazzled by the younger woman making dreamy eyes at him?'

'Oh, she dazzled him, no question. Just as much as he dazzled *her*, when all is said and done. But what I'm saying is that Max was not a philanderer at heart. He might have found his soulmate. What he experienced with Margo was what the French would call the *coup de foudre*, the thunder-bolt. He remained faithful to her for the rest of his days.'

'And what about Margo, was she as steadfast?'

'I would think so. I have to admit, I didn't know her all that well. We were all quite cordial with one another, just not close. After they got married, Max would spend a lot more time with her than with us colleagues, and he seldom mixed the two worlds. But I always got the impression she loved Max deeply and highly valued their relationship. I don't think there was any tiptoeing through the proverbial tulips on the part of either.'

Frank switched gears to see what might happen. 'What I'm interested in is if there might be anyone who had it in for them both. Anything come to mind for you through the years?'

Wootten ruminated, frowned, shook his head solemnly. 'Max had numerous run-ins on campus, but as I said, his university life never included Margo. And, well, those little donnybrooks are part of academia; they don't as a rule lead to murders. Not that all of us might not consider it in a moment of frustration.' He smiled at Frank, and noted the smile was not returned, so he sobered. 'Plenty of politics and infighting, don't get me wrong. But it's not like life and death. One thing about academic types, they tend to pride themselves on being highly civilized. I would hope people keep a certain perspective.'

'Returning to Paula — that was her

name? — seems like she could have had a grudge against them both. What happened to her?'

'A sad story. She passed away, not all that long after she and Max parted company in fact; maybe a year or so.'

'How did she die?'

'I'm not sure. I just remember when the word reached us of her death. She wasn't all that old. Max felt terrible. So did many of us who had known her. We were shocked.'

'Did she leave any family, any relatives?'

Wootten shrugged. 'Not that I know of. I think she was an only child, no siblings. She and Max didn't have any kids, of course. Max used to work for her father.'

'He worked for her father?'

'Yes, when I first met him and he was working towards his doctorate, he would put in a lot of hours with her father; he was . . . was it a plumber? No, an electrician, that's right. Max used to love to tell me stories of crawling around under buildings and falling out of windows. That was how he met Paula.

'I remember he said the old man was a widower; loved having him around to work and talk with; said he had always wanted a son. Max liked him; said he was a great guy. Then he got some security as a teacher, working towards professorial tenure, and was able to give that up.'

'And you don't know anything about the father?'

'I heard he passed away as well, nothing more.'

Frank had thought he saw a glimmer of a trail there, but it was elusive at best. Too long ago, everybody dead. Why couldn't it ever be simple? This problem was still going to have to be worried like a very tight knot.

'OK,' sighed Frank, flipping a page on his notebook. 'Let's talk about the tavern companions.'

The conversation with Wootten went on for nearly forty minutes. Max was clearly a happy subject for him. He described how Max progressively gave up his flamboyant pursuit of eternal youth and embraced a more appropriate guise as a wise mentor.

Max had actually chaired the department for a couple of years before tiring of the politics and deciding to return to teaching and publishing. Immediately thereafter he had produced two amazing pieces of scholarship that were applauded in the journals. Wootten himself had become department chairman and had held the position ever since. He had encouraged his old friend to continue full-time, but Max had decided he wanted to dial it back of late. That finally brought them back around to the original topic.

'So it was only in recent years that Max decided to cut back his hours and started getting moody over something?' Frank prompted.

'Yes. He started telling me that Margo had become strange; was growing distant from him and increasingly sarcastic. She made cryptic references. He said he had no idea what she was getting at, but she would act as if she expected he understood it. He said he was concerned she was having a nervous breakdown or early onset dementia or something along those lines.'

'Just curious here — did Margo work after they got married? What did she do?'

'To my knowledge, no, she stayed at home. Max made a decent living as a tenured professor with the prestige of several highly regarded published papers. I can't imagine Max would have minded if she had wanted to go to work, say to teach. She always had said she was brilliant. So I have to believe that Margo didn't want to do that.'

'No kids, right?'

'No children. They had a pet now and then. Max liked dogs. I suppose those were their surrogate children.' He noticed Frank's odd stare and continued, 'I had two children myself. They've grown and moved away.'

Frank couldn't resist asking, 'Just wondering — how did your wife feel about your hanging out with Max and your other colleagues back in those days?'

'My wife *is* a colleague.' He grinned. 'Teaches in the department. She even hung out with us when she could.'

Frank nodded. 'So all of a sudden Margo began to descend into some kind of abyss, according to Max.'

'Apparently.' Wootten shrugged. 'All I

knew was the progress reports he would bring us. He started showing up more regularly at the tavern.'

'What's the name of the tavern, by the way?'

Wootten winced. 'The Boar's Head. They purposely did that to attract the literary crowd. A little obvious for my taste.'

Frank nodded. 'Like in Shakespeare.'

Wootten smiled broadly. 'You're a reader then,' he commented with a nod.

'Some policemen do that,' Frank admitted. 'But now I'm digressing. Max — he was showing up more often at the tavern; things at home were going downhill?'

'Yes. Finally he said she had moved out. He seemed a curious mix of heartbroken and relieved. It was like that other shoe had finally fallen.'

'Did he mention anything about her threatening or harassing him?'

'Oh yes, that's right. Thomas Mann was poisoned. He came home one night to find the poor thing. He loved that dog. I think it was some solace for him after losing Margo.'

'Did he mention anything else?'

'He said Margo had taken to calling him regularly, making bizarre accusations. He called her increasingly irrational.'

'When I spoke with him he mentioned something about her trying to break into his condo.'

'Yes, he mentioned that as well. Said someone had jimmied his door lock or something like that. I don't think he had much of a grasp of how a lock works or what would be done to open it. We all felt he was being overly dramatic.'

'But yet someone did poison his dog.'

'Yes. I suppose that could have been Margo. If she really was losing it.'

'Was Max seeing a doctor? Could he have had, say, a heart condition?'

Wootten thought this over. 'Come to think of it, he was taking some kind of pills, or at least he took some once or twice while we were together. But I have no idea what they were.'

They talked for a few more minutes but it seemed to Frank he was starting to come around full circle now, and at least for the moment he was finished here. He took the names of the two other academics who made up the 'tavern companions' and bid Wootten farewell with a thanks and a hand-shake.

'I hope you find whoever did this horrible thing,' Wootten said gravely.

'I will,' replied Frank.

★   ★   ★

He decided he didn't want to bother Monica again today. He had more questions now about Margo's married life, but they could wait. For now, he would drive back to the squad room and take stock.

Frank's mind raced as he drove. He liked to make lists in his head, and by now it was second nature for his brain to construct them almost subconsciously as he navigated his vehicle through traffic.

Margo could have killed Max but Max could not have killed Margo.

More likely they were both killed by the same person.

Somebody would have needed suffi-cient reason to kill them both.

'It's her fault.'

'It's his fault.'

What was that supposed to mean?

Both harassing each other? Or somebody else harassing them both and making them think it was each other?

Why?

In his mind's eye, he circled that last question over and over and over.

Something's wrong about this whole thing.

You couldn't make it look as if they killed each other — that was impossible — but that was what it looked like someone was trying to do.

Why?

Something's missing. In frustration, Frank hit the steering wheel with the palm of his hand.

5

Frank thought again about how television police shows never seemed to show police personnel filling out paperwork. It seemed like the major part of every real-life cop's job was doing just that. There were reasons for it, and Frank understood them well. At some point, there needed to be a legitimate chain of evidence that could be taken to trial and not shredded by skilful defense attorneys or rejected by exasperated judges. Every officer and every detective was constantly reminded that the care they exercised in establishing that chain of evidence, documenting every interview and every action, could ultimately make the difference between conviction and acquittal. It all made sense. He just hated it. It seemed to take up more time than everything else he did in a day.

It also meant that he could expect at least some kind of preliminary reports from the techs and the coroners, and if he was lucky he'd get something before the weekend. Otherwise he'd be out of luck until at least Monday and likely beyond.

Waiting on his desk was a large manila envelope. It included summaries of the on-scene reports from Max Hesterberg's condo. He was still waiting on an autopsy and lab results, but at least this would give him something. He dumped the contents on his desk and pored through them. Death seemed pretty clearly to be from cardiac failure as the result of being electroshocked by a Taser. No indications of forced entry, theft or vandalism. The evidence suggested that Hesterberg had opened the door to someone who had then shot him with the Taser, watched him die, removed the darts and proceeded to depart, leaving the body blocking the door.

And, Frank remembered, *don't forget the attacker left the note:* IT'S HER FAULT.

He considered something, went to his computer and did a quick search. He thought he understood electroshock weapons but wanted to check to be sure. As he thought, Tasers were seldom fatal, but there were cases of deaths from them. One study specified that a shock from a Taser 'can cause cardiac electric capture and provoke cardiac arrest' and went on to describe exactly how. Wrongful death lawsuits, he was well aware, had been brought over Taser deaths. His own department was dealing with one at present.

Still, how could you be sure you'd kill somebody if you used one? Suppose you knew they had a heart condition? Would that make it a sure kill? He needed to know more about this, and made a note to consult someone.

Another thought occurred to him: what if the assailant's aim was *not* to kill Max? What if the intent was to disable him, put him out of commission for a length of time?

But why?

So he would be alive when Margo was killed, perhaps somehow implicated in her death?

That seemed pretty far-fetched.

Frank could find several problems with that scenario, not the least of which was those nasty burn marks on Hesterberg's chest from the darts that would provide a convincing alibi if he had survived. Things might not have gone as planned.

He shook his head. Going down this path was not productive. He needed better direction, something from the evidence. But the evidence was always slow in coming. Labs and medical examiners were always backlogged.

Sometimes it was good to be a dinosaur. He hadn't forgotten the value of the old methods. It was just that they were so tedious.

Now his desk phone was ringing, a call being put through from the front. He picked up the receiver and identified himself.

'You're the detective in charge of the Hesterberg murder?' It was a raspy woman's voice with a definite east-coast accent.

'Excuse me, which Hesterberg murder?'

'What are you, a wise guy? What do you mean which one?'

Frank rubbed his temple with his free hand. 'I'm sorry, and no, I am not being sarcastic. There are two and I'm working on both.'

A short silence. 'Max Hesterberg. The professor.' It sounded like the husky voice of an inveterate smoker.

'Yes, how can I help you?'

'I'm his sister, Angela. I've come to town to plan his memorial service. And hopefully to get some answers from you about what the hell happened.'

'I wish I could be of more help to you on that score, Miss Hesterberg — '

'Actually it's Mrs. Colletta.'

'Mrs. Colletta, I would actually like to see if you might be able to give *me* some information. I've only just begun the investigation, and there are a lot of questions.'

'And what's this about *two* Hesterberg murders? You're not talking about — '

'His wife, Margo Hesterberg. Unfortunately, yes. She was also murdered, just yesterday.'

'Oh my Lord!' came the exclamation over the phone. After a brief pause she repeated it. 'What is going on in this town?'

'I wish I could tell you. So you're in town now? Can we possibly talk today?'

'I'm here. Flew in from Pennsylvania. I'm being told Max's body can't be released so I can't plan a service yet. Is there anything you can do to help me there?'

'I doubt it. I'm sorry. They can't release him until there's been an autopsy. I'm hoping that will be done in the next few days.'

'I wish that didn't have to be done. Quite a violation to Max's remains, you know?'

'I understand, Mrs. Colletta, but you can understand it's necessary in this case.'

'Yeah, yeah. So I gotta play the waiting game here.'

'In the meantime, it really would be a big help if you could come talk with me.'

'Why not?' Angela muttered. 'Tell me where I'm going.'

Frank established her location and gave her directions and they agreed on an interview in an hour.

That gave him an hour to catch up on his own paperwork, he decided.

* ★ ★

Angela Colletta was a short woman with frosted hair and an expressive face. In person, her voice seemed even huskier. They were sitting in a drab interview room, drinking coffee from Styrofoam cups. Frank had apologized for the lack of amenities but she had waved it all aside. She struck him as a no-nonsense, down-to-earth type, which gave him some hope of helpful insights into Max and maybe even into Margo.

He had spent the first few minutes answering her numerous questions and informing her about the murder as much as he felt he could. She expressed almost equal concern as to the fate of Margo. It all seemed truly incomprehensible to her.

Frank finally decided it was time to turn the questioning around to her. 'Anything you might tell me about Max and Margo's relationship?'

'Well, it's not like Max and I have been in close communication over these years. We weren't on the outs or anything; we just . . . well, you know. You get busy with life and don't stay in touch. Can I smoke in here?'

'I'm sorry, no.'

'What is wrong with the world these days, can't smoke anywhere! But anyway . . . I knew Margo better in the early days, when I lived out here too. She and Max seemed so much in love. She seemed to be so good for him.'

'When they got married, you mean?'

'And afterward. When Max met her, he was in the middle of some kind of life crisis, you know? He was approaching forty, and how he dreaded that big birthday; it, like, symbolized the end of the world for him. He was doing a lot of that stuff that guys of a certain age sometimes do, you know? The clothes, the slang, everything but the red sports car! And we sometimes kidded him that that was next. I was worried when he met Margo and left his old girlfriend for her.'

'That would be Paula?'

'Right, Paula Graham. I figured this was just a phase, trading her in for a younger model, a trophy girlfriend kind of thing. Only it didn't turn out like that at all. Instead they were really great for each other. For a short time they ran around doing twenty-something stuff — going to concerts, poetry readings at coffee houses, that type of thing. Then they just kind of started settling in. Max started acting more his age. She was a very settling influence, that's a good word for her.'

'I'm told she was a brilliant student of literature.'

'I can't speak to that, but she was smart. Quick on the uptake. Kind of innocent in the ways of the world, but articulate. Very sweet, very charming. I sort of didn't want to like her when I first met her but I couldn't help it.'

'It sounds like she gave up her studies and any thought of a career to be with your brother.'

'You know, it was weird, but not only did Max seem to find everything he needed in her, she seemed to find everything she needed in him. Yeah. They became like a closed circuit. They both loved books, movies, poetry — they just fit together. There was their world alone and then there was their contact with the rest of the world. Over time the two overlapped less and less.'

Frank thought about what Mark Wootten had told him only a few hours earlier. The two seemed to have an idyllic marriage, at least for many years at the beginning.

'So you and Max both lived here at the time, that was about twenty-five years ago?'

'Longer. We both moved here from Pennsylvania to go to school. We established residency and went to State. Max got his degree in English and then his master's and his doctorate. I got a degree in sociology. I decided I didn't like it out here, and it got hard to find a job. I wound up moving back near home and becoming a social worker in Philadelphia, but that was some years later.'

'Max didn't go into teaching immediately after graduation?'

'Max wanted to be a perpetual student. He loved school; went right into a grad program. He wasn't sure he wanted to teach. He wanted to write.'

'So he ended up working to put himself

through, is that right?'

She laughed and made a face. 'Yeah, he went to work for an electrician, Roger Graham. I swear he was going to kill himself on that job. He fell out of a couple of buildings, got a few nasty shocks — once he got stuck under a building and had to be pulled out by firemen! He was a terrible electrician. I used to call him the Electrician's Apprentice, like *The Sorcerer's Apprentice*, that cartoon?' Frank nodded at her. 'But he took this pride in being a working man. A lot of college boys have this thing about being a working man, you know? And Roger paid him well and tolerated his incompetence.'

'Paula was his boss's daughter then. And she became his girlfriend.'

'I gotta tell you, I think she was a big reason that Roger kept him on the job. That, plus he liked Max. He looked at him sort of like a son. Other guys who worked for him, it wasn't the same. Max was special to Roger. If I recall, Roger's wife had died; he only had Paula. He really was looking forward to Max joining the family.'

'But he and Paula didn't marry, they just lived together?'

'Right. For a few years, in fact. Max was getting close to his doctorate and he was offered a position at the university, so he quit being an electrician before he got electrocuted, which was a good thing. Oh my God.' Angela stopped and put a hand up to her mouth.

'Mrs. Colletta?'

A tear formed in her eye. 'I just realized how Max actually died.'

As luck would have it, there was a box of tissues in the interview room. Frank found it and put it on the table in front of her.

'I am so stupid,' she said as she wiped her eyes and then blew her nose.

'No, you're not.'

'I'm just mad at myself for that dumb joke. Sorry for falling apart like this.'

'Perfectly understandable. Take your time.'

Angela recovered rapidly. No question she was a tough one. An urban social worker, Frank figured. She would have to be.

'Anyway, Max started teaching and he just took to it. He loved being around the students. As I said, by now he was in his thirties and starting to feel like he was going over the hill. He worked at his doctoral thesis for a couple more years before it was accepted. I think Roger missed having him at work, but Paula was still there and they all stayed fairly close.'

'Max never married Paula? No kids?'

'No.'

'I wonder what kept them together.'

Angela shrugged. 'Never made sense to me. I'd go over to visit them and they'd just, you know, be *there*. It wasn't like they hated each other — they were always kind of happy and nice — but it wasn't like they had a lot of visible affection for each other. Max was a restless kind of guy; he wanted to do stuff. She struck me as wanting to stay at home as much as possible.'

'She wasn't a student?'

'Oh no. Far from it. She did work for her dad. She'd do his book-keeping, file stuff, that kind of thing.'

'So it seemed to you that Paula was

more invested in the relationship than Max? You say he was starting to have this midlife crisis or whatever?'

Angela nodded with a grim smile. 'Couldn't have been easy for her. I loved my brother a lot, Detective; he was a great guy in so many ways. But to be honest, he was kind of a self-absorbed sort. He made a great academic in that way.'

'So Max met Margo and had a whirlwind romance.'

'That was so weird. As I said, I thought that was a doomed enterprise from the outset. I thought she was this starry-eyed young bimbo taken by her teacher and he was this aging fool full of self-doubt whose head had been turned by his pretty young student. That's how it must have looked to everyone.'

'Sounds as if they hardly acted discreetly.'

'Not exactly. It was a bit of a scandal.'

'So Max and Paula didn't last much longer.'

'No, she had moved out and was gone, and then Max and Margo were announcing their wedding.'

'And what happened to Paula?'

'I don't know for sure. Moved out of town somewhere, I think, and had no contact with any of us, which is understandable. Some time later the word got out that she had died, but there were never any details. Max tried to contact Roger but he couldn't locate him; his business had closed.' Angela paused for a moment and something seemed to light in her eyes. 'Do you think this is important in terms of Max's death? Is that why you're asking me about all this old history?'

Frank shrugged. 'I don't know, Mrs. Colletta. I'm trying to get as much background as I can. There's not an awful lot to go on. My thought is that someone bore a grudge against both Max and Margo, or maybe I should just say someone wanted them both dead. So far there's not too much I can learn about them in more recent times. I figure everything I can find out about them might be of some help.'

'Well, I left town about . . . ' She did quick computations in her head. 'I think it was nineteen years ago. As I said, I lost touch with Max and Margo. But up until then I saw them on a pretty regular basis.'

'Tell me a little bit about them in those years. I understand Max was a bit combative.'

'You mean at work? I heard a few stories, mostly from his point of view. He got impatient with what he called truculence. I mentioned he could be self-absorbed. There were times he couldn't understand why everyone else didn't readily fall in line with his opinions on everything.'

'So he had fights with other faculty members?'

'If you can call it fighting. If you ask me, professorial-type guys, they're all fuss and feathers. They're hung up that they're so cerebral, so they feel like they have to act macho. They drink together and argue and posture and puff up like pigeons. It doesn't mean anything. It's getting out their inner machismo. I honestly could not see any of those faculty gents committing an actual act of violence. I don't think they could have had a fistfight, much less kill one another.'

'I understand Max had a few run-ins with female faculty members, or administrators.'

'Could be. I'm not aware of anything specific, but Max would lock horns with anybody. I was going to make a joke and say, now, women on the faculty, you better watch out, they're secure enough, they *could* be killers; but under the circumstances that's a really bad joke and I wouldn't really mean it, so I better not.'

Frank caught himself rubbing the back of his neck. Angela said, 'What's the matter with me? I'm just not myself. I wish I hadn't said that.'

Frank let it go but told himself that he was rather glad she had said it. It was at least a slight confirmation of one of his own few angles.

Angela could not offer much insight on Max's life for the past fifteen to twenty years, though she said she had had a few intermittent telephone conversations with him in recent years in which he had informed her that Margo had moved out. He had been circumspect in their conversations, not volunteering much, but she had sensed his tone growing more unhappy and agitated. There was that same word again: 'agitated.' It seemed the term everybody who knew Max used to characterize him in recent times. Finally Frank felt that there was no more to be gained from extending the conversation.

Angela would be in town for a few more days at least, and there would be more opportunities to pursue any newer lines of enquiry. He exchanged contact information with her and asked to be informed when the service was scheduled.

She thanked him for his concern, but his true interest was to see who else might show up that he might get a chance to interview.

'And by the way,' she said as they shook hands, 'I think I'd like you to call me Angie, all right? I've decided you're OK. And to tell you the truth, I still never got used to being Mrs. Colletta. When people call me that I look around for Vinnie's mother, you know?'

★ ★ ★

118

Across the bustling squad room, Lieutenant Castillo caught Frank's eye and beckoned him into his office. 'How would you feel about overtime this weekend?' he asked. Frank shrugged. Actually he had been hoping for it.

'Why not?' he said. 'Does this have to do with the Hesterberg murders?'

Castillo nodded. 'Just spoke with Captain Crowley. We're getting a little bit of heat down the channels. After all, it's State University; my guess is there might be political ramifications, but you did not hear that from me. Plus it's a high-profile case now. Did you happen to see the television in the last hour or so?'

'Can't say as I have.'

'They found out about Margo Hesterberg and have been splattering it all over the afternoon news. It'd be best for us all if we can close these pretty quick.'

'It'd help if we could get prints, labs, coroner reports this weekend.'

Castillo nodded. 'I have a feeling there will be word coming down to all of them as well. But I can't promise anything. On the other hand, I know you. I can't think of anybody I'd rather have tracking this down. You've got the old-school skills.'

Frank twisted one corner of his mouth up into a wry smile and said nothing. He knew this was a reference to several comments he had previously made about younger detectives over-depending upon the science.

'So where do we stand on those cases right now?' the lieutenant asked.

'Not all that much to go on, Lou.' It was another running semi-joke between Castillo and his detectives that they constantly called him Lou, for Lieutenant. When he first took over the office he had been just a trifle self-important, and this was the veterans' way of clueing him in. He had grown in the job and earned a bit of respect by letting the little digs from his charges go by, as long as they kept the hierarchy in the proper perspective.

Frank continued: 'They both thought the other was harassing them in weird ways. I'm thinking it was a third party working on both of them who then killed them both. They led very private lives; not a lot in the way of personal histories. I've got a couple of leads but I have to admit they're slim.'

'Take whatever time you'd like this weekend, Frank. I got the word from the captain directly and I can authorize whatever you need. There will be people upstairs coming in to work on Monday who are going to want some news from me. Help me out here.'

An idea occurred to Frank. 'Maybe I can get you to move some of the rest of my caseload over to someone else?'

Castillo eyed him carefully. 'What do you have in mind?'

'Nothing all that major. I've just got these pain-in-the neck dead-end things that aren't going to go anywhere, we all know it, but I have to put in the time and the *due diligence* on them.' He punctuated that phrase sardonically, and then mentioned the cases by name. Castillo nodded. He knew exactly the cases to which Frank was referring. He heaved a sigh.

'You drive a hard bargain, Detective Vandegraf. OK. Bring me the files.'

'If I might make a suggestion, Lieutenant,' Frank added as he started to turn around, 'I think Detective Morrison is reasonably free right now.'

Castillo shot him a look. 'I'll take that under counsel, Detective. Good luck. Make sure I've got those files today before I change my mind. And bring me something I can use Monday. Please.' He dropped his gaze to the papers on his desk, signaling they were done.

Frank returned to his desk, navigating around hectic cops bustling to and fro with purpose. He contemplated his next move. He wasn't sure what he could do, but he knew he needed to keep in motion; to put in the time and see where he found himself.

He didn't want to return to speak with Monica Wersching until tomorrow at the earliest. Give her the night, at the very least, to deal with her grief. Anyway, he wanted to mull over what he had learned today to formulate new lines of questions for her. At this point she was the only source of information about Margo.

One matter had arisen while talking with Angie Colletta. It might be easy enough to track down. He sat down at his computer and began to search out death records for Paula Graham.

He had to admit, sometimes it was pretty great to live in the digital age. He remembered when he was a new fresh addition to the squad room and had to do searches the old-fashioned way, on the telephone or fax or more likely in person at the office of records. He had logged in lots of hours tracking down stray pieces of information. This was better, much better.

He estimated the year of her death around twenty-five years ago and navigated online, chasing down possibilities. There was only one death of a Paula Graham in the area and it had occurred in the town of Amberville, a couple hundred miles to the north. That sounded promising. A few more enquiries and he was able to pick up the phone and request a copy of the death certificate. The records office promised to email it through within the hour.

While he waited, he gathered together the relevant files for the cases he hoped Castillo would take off his hands and carried them to the lieutenant's office. He made a point to walk past Marlon Morrison's desk, humming softly to himself. Morrison looked up from a book he was reading at his desk and raised his eyebrows at him. Frank just smiled and nodded at Marlon.

The death certificate came through within a half hour, which surprised Frank. He always expected bureaucracies to work slower than promised, not faster, and was seldom disappointed in those expectations.

He opened the email attachment and enlarged it on his monitor. He found himself rereading the particulars several times, and then he printed it and reread it several more times.

Now he knew how Paula Graham had died. He cursed under his breath, not out of irritation but out of amazement. This added a whole new twist.

It was still a long shot but it was clearly the best he had.

Now he knew what he was going to be doing tomorrow.

6

Saturday morning, he got an early start and the drive to Amberville was reasonably pleasant. It was mostly open highway, along the coast, and he did the 185 miles in about two and a half hours.

Department policy mandated checking in with the local law enforcement as a courtesy, and the first thing Frank did was to search out the Amberville police. As luck would have it, when he arrived at the reception desk he was informed that the chief of police herself was in the station, and he was ushered into her office. Wilma Acosta was a heavyset woman in perhaps her mid-forties who rose from her desk to greet Frank affably. He introduced himself and showed his badge and identification, which she inspected carefully and handed back.

'How may I help you, Detective Vandegraf?' she asked, settling back at her desk and motioning to a chair for him to sit. He explained he was involved in a murder investigation and laid out his objectives as simply as he could.

She chewed over his story and nodded. 'That's a good one. You're thinking this might be an important clue leading to the murderer, then?'

'To be honest, it might be nothing at all. I may have come all the way up here on a wild goose chase, Chief, and I might just be heading back home right after. Or maybe it'll lead to something. It's all I've got at the moment.'

'How would you feel about my accompanying you, Detective? Not much going on around here right now, to tell you the truth, and this might turn out to be interesting. And maybe I can be of help finding your way around town.'

Not exactly what he had planned on, but when he thought it over, he really had no objections. At the very least, Chief Acosta could facilitate his search. He didn't really know what he was doing here, and maybe it wouldn't be so bad to have some-one to bounce ideas off of. He agreed and she stood up, grabbing her hat.

'I'd be happy to drive if that's OK.'

'Why not?' said Frank. 'Just let me get some things out of my car.' In a minute or two, he was climbing into Acosta's police cruiser, which was actually a late model SUV.

'So what you're looking for is Amberville General Hospital,' she said, putting the vehicle into gear and pulling out of the parking lot. 'Right up the road here. Changed a bit since back then — you did say twenty-five years ago?'

'Correct,' replied Frank, watching the road.

'But they ought to still have the records you're looking for, and maybe even someone who was there and remembers. Lots of older folk in this town.'

'You seem to know the town pretty well. How long have you been chief of police?'

'Going on ten years now. Succeeded my husband George.'

'He died?'

'Good lord no. Just retired. He's still sittin' at home, probably watching TV. Me, I like this job. I'll keep it as long as the people of Amberville let me.'

'So you've lived here all your life?'

'Not yet,' Wilma said, gunning her engine.

Shortly thereafter she announced they had arrived and pulled into a parking lot dominated by a large sign reading AMBERVILLE GENERAL HOSPITAL.

★   ★   ★

Amberville General's chief administrator was a cordial but businesslike woman named Alice Martin. Her office was small but tidy and surprisingly homey, with comfortable chairs and walls covered with photos.

She was tapping intently at a computer; the three were seated at a small conference table. Whatever misgivings she may have had about sharing the records in question had been swept away by Wilma's friendly assurances. Frank privately conceded that there was something to the way small towns ran. He was also glad that Wilma had come on board with him after all.

Alice swiveled the monitor screen to face Frank. He scanned what was on the

128

screen. It confirmed what he had already learned.

'Paula Graham died in childbirth,' he said simply.

'Yes, that's what our records indicate.'

Frank had already done the figures in his head. Paula left Max in March. Max and Margo were married in April. Paula Graham went into her fatal labor in early October.

'She was early. Her due date had been originally calculated for late November,' Alice said, peering over the top of her glasses at him.

'The child was premature. Did he or she survive?' Frank asked, trying to peruse the information on the screen.

Alice scrolled up and down. 'It would seem so, yes. At least the child survived birth.' She pointed to the monitor. 'Baby Boy Graham, it says here. Apparently the child hadn't yet been named.'

'Would there be records of the child, what happened to him?'

Alice shot a glance to Wilma, who gave a reassuring nod. She returned the screen to face her and tapped a few more keys.

'He was sent to Nightingale County Medical Center, where they had better neonatal intensive care resources. That's where our records end.'

'Any indication as to the father of the child?' Frank asked.

'The father was not named.'

'Did somebody bring the mother into the hospital, is that indicated?'

Alice carefully examined the information on the screen. 'It would seem it was her father. He's the only other person referenced.'

Wilma broke in. 'How about the physician who did the delivery?'

'Let me see . . . here we are. Handley Lucas.'

'I know Handley. He's been retired for a while now. He's still in town.'

'Yes. Actually his daughter took up his practice.'

Wilma looked quizzically at Frank. 'Think it's worth paying a visit to Handley and seeing if he remembers anything?'

'Possibly,' mused Frank. He looked back at Alice. 'How far away is Nightingale County Medical Center?'

'About a half hour, out Route 25. Wilma can direct you.'

'I wouldn't mind starting with Dr. Lucas. Can I get a number to call him?'

'Why don't you let me do that?' Wilma said, reaching for her own phone.

'Might make the whole thing go much smoother.'

★   ★   ★

It didn't take long for Wilma to locate Dr. Handley Lucas or to arrange to meet with him. He was a hearty seventy-something man, still possessed of a good head of snowy hair and a warm smile. When they arrived at his home, he looked happy to greet Wilma and to be introduced to Frank. They now sat at his kitchen table with mugs of fresh coffee, Frank's notebook open in front of him.

'Sure, I remember Paula,' Lucas recollected. 'Roger — her father — was a friend of mine. That's why she ended up in Amberville to begin with.' He shook his head. 'Very sad.'

'What can you tell me about her, the

whole situation?' Frank asked, leaning over intently. For some reason his gut feeling was telling him he was approaching something crucial to his case.

'Well, that was a long time ago. But I recall Roger calling me, saying his daughter needed a private place to bring her baby to term and then to deliver. We didn't talk about the whys and what-fors. She was in trouble and needed help, that was all I needed to know. I said of course. I found her a house for rent, she came up here, and I was her obstetrician for the course of her pregnancy.'

'Paula's father, Roger — did he come with her?'

'No, but he visited her quite often. He had his business to tend to, down your way.'

'You must have gotten to know her somewhat. Did you get any kind of sense of what was going on with her?'

'To be honest, I don't remember. I always had a lot of patients. Of course I tried to give them all my personal attention, but things tend to run together after so many years. And I do recall she wasn't very talkative; we never discussed much beyond her prenatal care.'

'No mention of who the father of the child was?'

'No, that was something that was avoided. She refused to name him at any point.'

'She went into premature labor, didn't she?'

'Specifically what happened was, she had a condition known as pre-eclampsia. It was necessary to induce birth to try to prevent it from progressing to full-out eclampsia, which can be extremely serious, resulting in seizures in the mother and even death. The baby was delivered very early. But as you know, the mother still didn't survive.'

'Was Paula's father here for the delivery?'

'Yes. He wasn't in the delivery room. We kept him out because of the complications of the procedure and the delivery, which was standard procedure. He was in the waiting room through everything.' Lucas again shook his head, this time with an expression of deep sadness even after all this time. 'I had to go and tell him what had happened. It just destroyed him.'

'What about the baby?'

'The baby survived, but being almost eight weeks premature, he was in danger. He was transported to Nightingale to their neonatal intensive care unit.'

'Do you have any idea what happened to the baby after that?'

'Oh yes,' Lucas said. 'He made it. Roger planned on taking his grandson back and raising him when he was out of danger. The baby had still not been named; he was just 'Baby Boy Graham' on the isolette in the NICU. Roger was going to name him Paul.'

'It sounds as if something else happened before he could do that,' Frank noted.

'I'm afraid so. There was an accident.'

'You mean Roger Graham had an accident?'

'Yes. He was working on the wiring for a building that was under construction. He was electrocuted. Died on the spot.'

'Right when he was about to bring his grandson home? Really?'

Lucas nodded sadly, briefly closing his eyes. 'He was trying to finish up the job so he could devote a few days up here to all the details when they discharged the boy. Maybe he was rushed and distracted because of everything that had happened. We'll never know. He was being a bit reckless, perhaps.'

Not much worse than a reckless electrician, Frank thought, but wisely kept it to himself. 'And the baby?'

'Nightingale County Social Services took custody. My understanding is he was put up for adoption. I have no idea what became of him. My wife and I briefly considered trying to adopt him ourselves, but we had four kids of our own, so it just wasn't a viable solution.'

'Did you try to follow the boy's progress?'

'It got complicated. He was transferred to somewhere else. I had some things come up here, both personal and my practice that monopolized my attentions for a long time. Apparently he was adopted in the interim — and those records, as you know, are confidential.'

'So it's conceivable he's a grown man today. He'd be about twenty-five.'

'Oh yes.'

'Would he have known about his birth mother?'

Lucas frowned. 'Maybe yes, maybe no. It's possible he wound up too many steps away in the system; too many degrees of separation, so to speak. There may have been nobody who could have told him anything whatsoever. Maybe his adoptive parents never even told him he was adopted. That happens.'

'He never came around here looking for information, to your knowledge?'

'No, not that I ever knew of. Sometimes I wondered whatever happened to him. But there was really no way I could investigate.'

Frank had been busily filling pages in his notebook throughout the conversation. He struggled to organize the whirlwind of thoughts and questions in his brain. 'There were no other relatives of the family surviving, no close friends?'

'Not that I knew of. Roger was a widower of some years. I don't think he even had any employees anymore, it was just him running the business. His daughter was all he had. And then his grandson.'

'But is it conceivable that the child could have learned the back story, who his mother was, what had happened?'

'I suppose. We're in the realm of complete speculation now, Detective. People go through their whole lives never knowing anything about their birth parents or where they really came from. A lot of people these days become intensely interested in exploring those things. Some of them find out their back stories. Just as many never do. Maybe some of it depends on how strong their desire is; to what lengths they're willing to go. But I tend to think it's mostly the luck of the draw.'

They talked a little longer and Frank asked every question he could think of. Lucas seemed willing to help as much as he could, but ultimately there was not much more he could provide. Finally Frank thanked him and he and Wilma said their goodbyes.

Outside the house Wilma told him, 'You look hungry. There's a good diner not far away, want to get a bite?'

'Read my mind, Chief. Any chance they have good pastrami?'

'Corned beef OK? Their coffee's decent too. And good pie.'

* ★ *

They were sitting in a booth in the diner, finishing their meal. Wilma said: 'You can go ask into adoption records over at the county seat, but I think you know that's likely a fool's errand. They are *very* vigilant about that kind of thing. You'd need to get a court order. You can get one, I'm sure, but not today.'

Frank rubbed the bridge of his nose with two fingers. 'I don't even know if this is really leading anyplace to begin with. It's still the best shot I seem to have so far.'

'Any other promising directions?'

'Not really. The victim crossed swords with a couple other individuals, but they're not the murderous type as far as I can tell. They don't feel all that right.'

'Everybody's the murderous type, given the right circumstances. That's my experience. Not yours?'

'No, you're right about that. But you know that *feel* you develop? Some things feel right for reasons you can't explain.'

'Oh sure.'

'And some things don't feel right, also for reasons you can't explain.'

Wilma took a sip of coffee and nodded sagely. 'I've learned to trust my hunches. You do this long enough, there's something that sinks down inside you, some process. Can't explain it, can't analyze it, but more often than not it's right on the money.'

'Yeah, I guess so.' Frank nodded. Leave it to another cop, however far removed from him, to get the point.

Wilma continued the thought. 'And something about this feels right for reasons you can't explain?'

'Maybe it's just that I have nothing else. I don't know. I can't put my finger on it yet.'

'I'd say trust your gut. And keep moving.'

'I guess that's good advice. I better get going.' He nodded to the waitress for a check.

'My treat,' Wilma said. 'This is the most interesting day I've had on the job in a while.'

He thanked her, finished his pie and coffee, and figured he'd better get on the long drive home. There wasn't much more he could do here and his time was better spent there. Wilma gave him a lift back to his car at the station.

While gassing up for the return trip, he phoned Monica and asked if she was up to having another conversation with him. She seemed amenable and they set up a tentative meeting in three hours. The entire drive back down the coast, Frank allowed his brain to spin freely, giving it rein to develop patterns.

Allow certain assumptions for the moment. First assumption: Max Hesterberg was the father of Paula Graham's child.

Second assumption: Max never found out that he was a father. She learned she was in early pregnancy and left without telling him.

Third assumption: the kid survived, grew up, and discovered the story of his original parents. The whole wretched story, rife with disappointment and abandonment and tragedy.

Large jump to the scenario for the fourth assumption: many years later the son seeks out and finds his father and the woman for whom his mother was thrown over, and seeks vengeance.

He tossed the story around in various permutations and variations. There were a lot of assumptions that couldn't be substantiated. That was always a danger, to be lured off on this kind of snipe hunt without evidence.

But it was all he had so far. And something about it felt strangely right.

The trip flew by rapidly as he became fully involved in his various hypotheses. He was ten miles away from the city when he realized he didn't even remember most of the drive. It was a bit alarming to think he had been driving on automatic pilot almost all of the way.

* * *

'I appreciate your letting me come by to talk again,' Frank was saying. They were sitting once again in Monica's front parlor. 'How are you doing?'

'I'm not sure it's truly set in as of yet,' she said. She seemed extremely subdued. 'They won't release Margo's body, either. I can't even plan a funeral or memorial yet.'

'I know. I'm sorry. I hope you understand.'

'I wish they didn't have to, you know . . .'

'Do an autopsy? Yes. But it's necessary, I'm afraid.'

'If it helps you to find whoever killed her, I suppose it's all for the best. Do you know how long it's going to take?'

'Maybe just this weekend, but I really don't know. It's not in my hands.'

'So ask me your questions. Maybe this will help me accept the reality of it all.'

'Are there any other family or friends who might be coming in for services?'

'No other relatives. Just me. Hadn't I mentioned that before? And friends, well, I'm not sure who Margo might have known. As far as I know lately, again, there's just me.' She laughed mirthlessly.

'And those apartment managers, for what they're worth. I don't know that she had any contact with anyone else whatsoever.'

'She wasn't close with them, though?'

'Oh heavens no. Why would she be? I was just making a joke.'

'Margo had no contact with anyone she might have known through Max?'

'Not in a long time. I think she was suspicious of everybody that had anything to do with Max. She avoided them, I'd say.'

'You said that she commented she came to believe Max was not the man she thought, something like that?'

'Yes, she said something like that quite often.'

'Any idea what that might have meant? Did she find out some specific information about him, maybe something in his past?'

'She would never go into specifics with me.'

'You never asked her, never pressed her on details? You weren't curious?'

'Oh of course I was, but Margo would never talk about things like that.'

'Did she suspect he was having an affair, seeing other women?'

'Again, there was never anything specific. I wondered about that myself, but their history was that they both were faithful to one another. I just don't know.'

'Did she ever mention anything about anybody contacting her, telling her things about Max perhaps?'

Monica thought about that one for a moment. 'No, not that I can recall.'

'So these just struck you as kind of free-floating concerns on her part, nothing that she had uncovered distinct details about?'

Monica pondered some more. 'I keep telling you, there was something. She wasn't crazy.'

'Did she ever talk about Max's life before she met him, his former girlfriend, anything like that?'

'Years ago she told me that the old girlfriend was dead, that was about it.'

'No details, like how she might have died?'

'I got the feeling they didn't know. She had just disappeared, and then one day someone said she had died.'

'Margo didn't really know her, I gather.'

'No, she maybe met her at some social engagement once or twice. Max went to great lengths to keep them separated, I think, and that was fine with Margo. I can't imagine the old girlfriend had any interest in meeting Margo either.'

'Do you think it's possible there could have been a child in Max's past? Was there anything that Margo might have said to that effect?'

'Max fathering a child? Wow, that would have been something.' The idea seemed incomprehensible to her.

'I'm just throwing out possible questions, Monica. So I guess the answer to that would also be no.'

'It would have been a huge surprise to me.'

'So Margo wasn't always so unhappy in her marriage, right?'

'My God no. They were the happiest people together I ever saw; downright smug in their private world.'

'Can you pinpoint the time when Margo

started becoming concerned about Max, when she started telling you about being upset?'

'Well, it all came to a head not quite a year ago when she moved out, but it had been building before that.'

'What I'm looking for is if there was some event that triggered all this to begin with, like one day out of the blue when Margo's troubles seemed to begin.'

'I can't answer that, Detective. I can't answer any of that.'

The conversation ended and he thanked her. As he walked to his car, the frustrating feeling of futility rose up once again. It was getting late in the day and once again his wheels were spinning uselessly.

What else could it be? It had to be the child. It had to be.

He couldn't think of much else he could do that evening. He could only hope tomorrow would be better.

7

It was late Sunday morning. After a fitful night, Frank had finally managed to fall asleep and to stay that way for a few hours. He was awakened by his buzzing cell phone and reached over to sleepily answer, 'Yeah.'

An unfamiliar male voice asked, 'Hello, is this Detective Vandecamp?'

'Vandegraf,' he corrected. 'Yes, this is Frank Vandegraf.'

'Detective, my name is Gary Rossi. Angie Colletta gave me your number. She said you might be interested in hearing what I knew about Max Hesterberg.'

Frank sat up in bed, now fully awake. 'You knew Doctor Hesterberg?'

'Yeah, I sure did. He and I worked together for Graham Electric back in the day. I was very saddened to hear of his death. She got in touch with me when she came into town. If I can do anything to help you find who did this, I'll be glad.'

'You might be a big help, actually. Is there somewhere we can meet?'

'Yeah, I'm near Goff Boulevard. There's a place near here I hang out at, you want to meet me there?'

'They have food?' asked Frank. He was hungry, and it seemed early to be visiting a bar, though that was clearly what Rossi had in mind.

'Sure. Nothing fancy. Sandwiches, chili, burgers, things like that.'

'Reasonably quiet?'

'Usually on Sundays, yeah.'

'Tell me where it is, I'll be there.'

'What time is good for you?' Rossi asked.

'How about right now?'

* * *

Frank gauged Rossi as being perhaps a bit older than Max Hesterberg would have been, a lifetime working man, wearing a denim shirt and black jeans. They met outside the establishment, which proved, as he suspected, to be a neighborhood bar. At least it was almost empty and quiet. Rossi looked as if he had spent a lot

148

of hours inside of bars like this. His heavy-lidded eyes had a weary quality. They found a booth and Rossi motioned to the bartender, who clearly knew him well, asking for a couple of menus. They ordered sandwiches and Rossi ordered a beer. Frank demurred on that and asked for coffee.

'You should see this place at night.' Rossi smiled, as if apologizing for it.

'So, Mr. Rossi, you wanted to talk to me about Max Hesterberg.'

'Yeah, I couldn't believe it when I heard what happened to him.'

'You said Angie Colletta told you about it.'

'Well, actually I first heard about him on the news, on TV. Then out of the blue I got a call from Angie, who I haven't seen or talked to in maybe fifteen, twenty years.'

'How exactly did she find you?'

'Phone book, I guess,' Rossi said. 'Or however you find telephone numbers these days. I still got a phone — I mean like a land line; I'm in the book or whatever.'

'So she remembered you.'

Rossi smiled. 'She used to flirt with me back in the day, when she was a smart little college girl. Had a thing for blue-collar guys, I guess. I always liked her.'

'Sounds like she knew you pretty well.'

He waved a hand rapidly. 'Oh no, nothing like that. She was Max's little sister; we just joked around and kidded each other a little. I was married at the time too.'

'So how long did you and Max work together?'

Rossi thought about it, looking belabored. 'Let's see. Roger brought him on as a helper, kind of an apprentice, when we got a spate of work and he felt he needed another hand to help out. I had been working there for a year or two at the time. Roger really liked Max. Well, I did too. He was a good guy, made a lot of jokes but took the work seriously. Smart guy, really smart. Liked to drink, which made him popular with us too. I must have worked with him for maybe two years before I left.'

'You left before Max?'

Rossi looked down at his beer and was silent for a long moment. 'I sort of had to. I got arrested.'

'Arrested for what?'

'Let me back up a little here. I told you I was married? Well, we had a few arguments. A few fights. I was going out and drinking a bit too much. I got in a coupla barroom fights and got hauled in. Someone swore out an assault complaint against me. Roger decided he'd had enough with me and he fired me after that.'

Frank just nodded.

'Uh, I'm not sure that Angie knows that part — don't tell her, OK? She just remembers me as this nice friendly guy who used to kid around with her.'

'No problem.'

'Anyway, after I settled all that legal stuff and went through a divorce, I found another job as an electrician, and sometime later Roger and I got to be friends again. Bygones and all that. He wouldn't hire me back but he'd sometimes get together with me for a beer. Once we even went to a ball game.'

'You say you knew Max for a couple of

years. Tell me what you know about him.'

'He would tell me how he was working on his degree — writing his thesis, he called it. He loved to read; he'd constantly tell me about some book or writer. I kinda got a kick out of it. Usually those egghead types look down their noses at people who actually work for a living. You'd go to do a job for some *professional* and they'd talk down to you and watch you like they didn't trust you weren't gonna steal something, stuff like that. Max wasn't like that. He was real people. I could see he was gonna go someplace, as they say.'

'Did you know much about his personal life?'

'I knew he and Roger's daughter had hit it off and they were going out. She was kind of a strange bird.'

'How do you mean?'

'Well, she was pretty cute — certainly nothing wrong with her on that score — but I don't think a lot of guys showed much interest in her, at least not past maybe a date or two. She was real shy. She finished high school and took a year

152

or two at community college.

'Roger had her working for him, keeping the books and taking phone calls and like that, so she was in the office a lot. That's how she and Max got to know each other. I think Roger was tickled to death that she liked Max and he liked her. He might have been worried that she was some kind of wallflower who would have ended up alone. Roger really liked Max; I think he was looking forward to having him as a son-in-law.'

'Was it while you were there that Max and Paula moved in together?'

'Oh yeah. I kidded him about that. At first Roger wasn't real happy with that arrangement, but he saw that Paula seemed so happy with Max, I guess he decided it would be OK.'

'I hear Max wasn't much of an electrician.'

Rossi laughed loudly, the most energy he had so far displayed. He shook his head as if recalling a favorite joke. 'At heart he was a college boy,' he said, clearly with affection. 'Roger sure didn't keep him on for his skills. He was never going to be a certified electrician. There were only certain things he was allowed do as an uncertified assistant, and he still managed to almost kill or seriously injure himself a few times.'

'Roger knew Max was going to leave one day. He was working on his doctorate.'

'Yeah, of course. Max never misled him on that score. They were honest with each other.'

'Until they weren't.' Frank watched Rossi carefully.

Rossi just shrugged. 'I was long gone by the time all that happened. I heard the story from Roger later, when we reconciled.'

'What was Roger's take on everything?'

'Max got offered a job as a teacher of some kind and quit. Roger was OK with that because Max would still be, like, in the family. He was very proud of Max and would brag about him to everyone he knew. He was still figuring they'd get married, have kids. But then Paula told him that she thought Max was seeing another girl. Stuff started happening real fast — they had some blow-up fights; Paula left. That was the story.' Rossi spread his hands.

'Did Roger ever tell you what happened after that?'

'Yeah. She was pregnant.'

Frank was dumbfounded for a long few moments. 'You knew about that?'

'Sure. One night Roger and I got fairly drunk and he told me.'

'I didn't know that anybody actually knew about that.'

'I don't think he ever told anybody else. Like I said, he was pretty drunk. I don't know if he even remembered ever telling me.'

'What else did he tell you?'

'Just that she didn't want to tell Max, so he sent her off somewhere to have the baby. That's all I know. I made a point of never bringing up the subject again with Roger. We only saw each other a few more times before he died. You know about that, right?'

'I heard it was an accident.'

'Yeah, story I got was he was up in this new construction and got killed. I hadn't seen him in a while, and heard the word one night. Too bad. I later heard that his daughter had died too, but that was a vague kind of a rumor; I never learned if it was true.'

'And you never looked into it?'

Rossi spread his hands. 'Well, to tell you the truth, I got myself in some more trouble right about then. I had kind of a full plate, if you know what I mean.'

'Back to jail?'

'Coupla fights, drunk and disorderly. I spent a little time in jail. Not prison, not the penitentiary, nothing like that. Just piddly stuff. After that I just got out, moved on. Decided to keep my nose clean and work. Got married again.'

'How'd that work out?'

'And divorced again.'

'Sorry.'

'And married again and divorced again. It's like lather, rinse, repeat.' He looked sad and weary, like an aging basset hound.

'Mr. Rossi, did you ever tell anyone else about Paula, about her pregnancy, any of that?'

'No, I thought it needed to be kept

private out of respect for the dead. In fact I kinda forgot about it. Oh. There was just that one guy.'

Frank almost dropped his pencil. 'What one guy?'

'About maybe two years ago. Guy calls me out of the blue and asks if I used to work for Roger Graham. Says his father was an old friend and he just wanted to find out what had happened to him.'

'How did he find you?'

'Search me. I figured Roger had mentioned me to the guy's father way back when. It was all kinda vague.'

'You didn't ask who he was or anything?'

He gave a sheepish grin. 'Well, I guess I had been drinking a little bit.'

Frank resisted the urge to bury his face in his hands. 'And what exactly did you tell him?'

'I got caught up in talking about old times. I guess I told him the whole story, what I knew of it. He seemed really interested; said his father would have been very upset to learn his friend was dead. He asked me about working with Roger.'

Frank took a deep breath. 'You told

him about Paula being pregnant?'

'I might have. Don't really remember.'

'You told him about Max?'

'Yeah, probably.'

'You told him about Max leaving Paula for a new girlfriend?'

'I might have, I don't remember. We were just talking, you know? Maybe gossiping a little.'

Frank could see that even after one beer Rossi was quickly getting a little sloppy. He could imagine him after 'drinking a little bit.'

'And you have no idea who this guy was? Who this father he was talking about might have been?'

'Like I said, I'd been drinking. It was a real friendly conversation. The guy was very — whattaya call it? — engaging. It was like we had met up in a bar, even like this one.' He waved around the room grandly. Then he looked morose again. The slouchy hangdog look returned. 'That's maybe why I remember anything about it. I miss stuff like that. Not a lot to laugh about these days. Not a lot of good memories to share about old friends. That was a fun conversation. I invited the guy to come join me for a drink, but he said he had to get going, maybe some other time.'

'Good memories,' muttered Frank.

'Sorry, missed that, what'd you say?' said Rossi.

'Nothing,' replied Frank. 'Did this guy happen to give his name?'

'Don't remember,' Rossi said with a weak smile. 'I had been — '

'I know,' said Frank, shutting his notebook. 'Drinking.' He started to get up. 'Thank you for your help, Mr. Rossi.'

'You know, I'm thinking I know why Angie got in touch with me,' Rossi said. 'I think she wanted to get together, you know what I mean? She said something about a husband back in Jersey or Pennsylvania or someplace. I think she wasn't in a hurry to get back to him, get my meaning?' He tried to wink but was even having trouble with that.

As Frank departed the dingy neighborhood saloon, he thought, *There are smart people. There are stupid people. And then there's Gary Rossi.*

He sat in his car mulling it over. It was increasingly clear: he had to get those adoption records. But there was no way to get them on a Sunday. In this state, law enforcement agencies generally were able to obtain copies of most public records, but adoption records were different. They were sealed after an adoption was finalized and could usually only be accessed by a court order. He could get that, but the process could take a couple of days. He had a feeling he didn't have much time. The murderer would likely not hang around for very long, if indeed they were even still here. For all he knew, the window of opportunity had already closed.

Once again his phone buzzed, and he dug it out to answer.

'You know, your voice is deeper on the phone than in person, Detective.'

'Chief Acosta. What a surprise.'

'You can call me Wilma. Can I call you Frank?'

'Wilma, if you're calling with some

kind of unexpected news, you can call me anything you want.'

'So I didn't get you at a bad time. Glad to hear it. I took a little trip over to the city of Nightingale last night and asked around a little bit. Figured you wouldn't mind, and things are pretty quiet here.'

'I only wish things ever got that quiet here.'

'City mouse, country mouse, you know that story?'

'Sure.'

'Anyway, I've got friends who work in the hospital and at the courthouse. Hunted down a pretty remarkable lady; she must be ninety. Her name's Helen Troy.'

'Helen of Troy? That would make her old indeed.'

'No 'of,' wise guy. Just Helen, space, Troy. She worked in social services for most of her life. She actually remembered Baby Boy Graham.'

'You gotta be kidding me.'

'Well, here's the thing. She arranged the adoption. They were in-laws.'

'Tell me you're making this up!'

'Small towns, Frank. Everybody knows everybody. Everybody winds up related to everybody. You come up to a place like this to get lost, but what you do is get known.'

'Do I need to come back up there?'

'Naw, not worth it. I can tell you the sum total of what I was able to learn. It's not like she could tell me a whole lot. Just enough, I hope.'

Frank had his notebook out at the ready. He was almost trembling with excitement and had to catch himself.

'Baby Boy Graham was adopted by Joseph and Anna Benecke. They lived in the city of Nightingale.' She spelled it for him.

'You say they're this lady Helen's in-laws?'

'Were. Past tense. They are gone, may they rest in perpetual light. Not close relatives, it would seem. Her husband didn't get along with his sister — that was Anna. It would seem that Joe and Anna were decent enough, but a little eccentric and kind of a pain to get along with.'

'And they adopted the boy?'

162

'Yep. Helen said the kid's name was something like Arnold or Ernie or Emile or something like that. That's really all she had. Helen's reasonably sharp for a nonagenarian, but she tends to ramble. I had to sit through a lengthy recitation of her family tree and friends and their friends, all sorts of side trips to get that much.'

'What happened to them? Any idea?'

'She's almost positive they're dead. She has no idea what became of the kid. He'd be about twenty-five now.'

He scribbled furiously on the notebook in his lap. 'I'd guess anything else I need to search for, I can do from here.'

'That's kinda what I figured. So calling you Frank is OK then?'

'Wilma, I owe you big. I'll come up and buy you dinner some night.'

'Just don't tell George, my husband. Talk to you later.'

Frank started his car. His next destination was the squad room, his computer and maybe even old-fashioned telephone books — anything at his disposal. With luck he might just be able to access information, even on a Sunday, for people named Benecke in that area.

★ ★ ★

Sometimes this digital age wasn't such a bad thing after all, he considered. He sat at his desk staring at his computer screen. The squad room was fairly quiet at the moment, only a few detectives on duty around the station.

It had taken some time navigating around and following one lead to the next; he was still not totally adept at this. But he thought he might have lucked out. The name in front of him, and the recently added post office address, could have had a flashing neon marquee around it and would not have stood out any more to him. Things clicked into place in his mind.

He grabbed his car keys and got to his feet.

★ ★ ★

'Detective, don't you ever take a day off over there at the police department?'

Super Judy stood in her doorway and stared balefully at Frank. Inside the apartment, over her shoulder, he could see her husband Steve sitting on the sofa with a beer, watching the television and casting annoyed glances over to the doorway.

'Sorry to disturb you, but I just have a couple quick questions for you.'

'Well, let's get it over with, then.'

'The other day when I was here you had a guy helping you out; I think he was moving the trash bins out to the street.'

'Yeah, Emil. What about him?'

'Do you happen to know his last name?'

Judy shook her head. 'Yeah, it's, uh . . . Hey Steve!' she called out. 'Emil's last name. It's like Becker, or — '

'Benecke, maybe?' Frank interrupted.

'Yeah, that's it. Why?'

'How do you know him?'

'He came around looking for work one day. Just rang our bell; said he was going all over the neighborhood since he'd just moved in close by. He's real handy. Good worker. Steve said he'd hire him on a job-by-job basis.'

'How long has he been working for you?'

'Oh, let me think. Less than a year, I'd say.'

'Could you connect it to something else to pin it down? Say, maybe, was it after Margo Hesterberg moved in here?'

'Definitely after that. One of his first jobs was to help us dispose of the stuff we took out and stored when we cleaned out the garden apartment to rent it to her.'

Steve had gotten up from the couch and joined Judy at the door. He hadn't let go of his beer. 'You're asking about Emil? Is he in trouble or something?'

'I just need to find him to talk to him. What do you know about him?'

Steve shrugged. 'Quiet guy, doesn't talk much. Pretty smart. Knows how to do all sorts of things. He didn't have a résumé or anything like that, but he told me he worked in a hardware store, as a locksmith, as a watch repairman, as a general handyman; he was even a building manager once.'

'Ever talk about his personal background?

Where he's from, anything like that?'

'He doesn't talk about himself much, but he did say he was from somewhere up north. He remarked he wasn't used to a big city like this one.'

'Do you have an address for Emil?'

'I'm not sure,' Steve said, looking dubious.

'He works for you, you have to pay him, you have to have information for him. You have to be able to get in touch with him to come over when you need him.'

'Well, we usually pay him in cash. But yeah, let me look.' Steve walked into the kitchen and returned with a card that might have been tacked on a bulletin board or stuck to the refrigerator with a magnet. It was covered with scrawls in pen. 'Yeah, got his number and an address.'

'I'm going to need this,' Frank said, taking the card. It bore a phone number with an out of town area code; the same code, he recalled, as Nightingale County. There was also an address only a few blocks away.

'I'll need that back,' Steve said.

Frank just nodded. If he was right, Steve and Judy wouldn't be needing this anymore, but he saw no need to mention that. 'Emil hasn't said anything about leaving town or anything like that, has he?'

Judy, who had been taking all this in with her eyes and mouth agape, shook her head. 'He's supposed to help us do some painting starting tomorrow. And as soon as we get the OK from you guys, we're going to start clearing out the garden apartment to re-rent it.'

Frank gave the address another look and pocketed the card. He looked at them both, trying not to show his excitement. 'Thanks for your help. No big deal going on, I just need to ask Emil a few questions. Enjoy the rest of your Sunday.'

He hustled back to the elevator and out to his car.

It made too much sense. It had to be the guy. Frank had noted that Emil had even worked as a locksmith.

The only thing he couldn't figure out was why Emil was still hanging around. If he had committed the murders, why wasn't he in the wind? Did he need to get back into the apartments? They were both sealed crime scenes at the moment. He was also confident that nobody knew who he was, so he felt that he had time. Maybe that was it. He had to feel his work was done, didn't he? He had agreed to come back to work tomorrow. Why hadn't he run yet?

'Pretty smart,' Steve had characterized him. 'The guy knows a lot.' Frank was familiar with a particular type of killer along this line. *He prides himself on his intellect. He figures he's several steps ahead of all of us and doesn't have anything to worry about, so no need to hurry; he can safely lag back and savor watching us spin our wheels. The kind of guy with the audacity to leave a calling card at each of his murders:* IT'S HER FAULT and IT'S HIS FAULT.

A man capable of two cold-blooded killings.

Frank picked up his phone and called for backup at the address.

8

In a cramped apartment, a lone man sat pensively in a darkened room, the only source of light coming from a television screen. The shades were drawn tightly against the outside world, though he assured himself he felt no fear whatsoever. Nobody out there could hurt him. They didn't even know who he was. But despite his self-assurances, he was nervously shaking.

The television news (which seemed to always be on *some* channel or other, no matter what time of day or night) was still featuring breathless reports on the two shocking murders of the previous week. A series of big-haired, bubble-headed personalities stressed that the police seemed to have no clues or information on the identity of the murderers, though there was speculation they were connected.

He found it interesting that there was no mention of the notes that had been left. Certainly they had found them. He had read that they — the police — liked to withhold certain evidence from the public, as a way of counter-checking the veracity of wannabe witnesses or those crazy people who just wanted to confess to crimes they had nothing to do with. That must be what was happening now, he figured. People, he reflected, could certainly be deranged.

He had been monitoring the news regularly to see if anyone was on to him. Not that he thought they ever would be. He had been clever. His plan had been perfect, if he did say so himself. They'd never figure it out.

Tomorrow he'd check his post office box; his regular check ought to be there as it always was on Mondays, and he could leave. He was still considering where he would go next. Not back home. There was nothing there for him anymore; it was no longer *home*. He'd go somewhere far away.

His current thought was Florida. He liked the pictures he had seen, all those palm trees and beaches. With all of his skills, he could get a job there; and between that and his regular checks, maybe he could save up enough to go to Europe. He'd always wanted to see Europe.

He wondered why he didn't feel better, now that he had accomplished what he had set out to do. For so long now, it had been eating away at him as he planned it and took each step so carefully. How many times had he almost lost patience, was tempted to throw caution to the winds and act impetuously, just so that those gnawing feelings in his gut would go away? But he was too smart for that. He forced himself to calm down and go slowly.

Why didn't he feel better now? he wondered. He felt terrible. The stomach ache was still there, the shaking apprehension all over his body.

His notes were right: it was all their fault. He had taken care of that. The fear, the aches should all have gone away as he was utterly convinced they would. Dad had always taught him to stay calm, think before he acted, think thoroughly, plan for every eventuality. Dad promised that would always lead to success. Dad taught him to investigate, to learn precisely how things worked, to be methodical in his approach: how to navigate the intricacies of watches, of locks, of all manner of machinery.

But of course that wasn't really his dad. Maybe everything he had taught him was wrong then.

He remembered finding out that they weren't his parents. They told him not long before they died. He remembered how it had turned his life upside down, changed something inside of him.

It had taken a long time, but he had pieced together his own story, the hidden history that he had been forbidden to know until then. It infuriated him that he had been kept in the dark all those years. No, he had been *lied* to by people he trusted.

So of course they deserved to die. They were old; he just sort of helped them along.

He wished he had known his real mother. He had come to picture her in his mind: beautiful, wise, kind and loving. She would never have lied to him, never. She was a martyred saint. Her very love for him, for her son, had killed her.

He wished he had known his grandfather. He had a mental picture of him as well: ruggedly handsome, long-suffering, and supportive. Had the two of them only lived, his only real family, what a life he could have had!

It was not their fault they had died, his mother and grandfather. He had learned that in his journey as well. The procedure worked: investigate, observe, learn how things work. Wait until you know everything. It was a slow process, small steps, discovering the names of his mother and grandfather, tracing them back to the city. He was intensely proud of himself for unearthing the information about Roger Graham's business, tracking down an old employee, playing his role perfectly, and learning the key information that had led him to his birth father.

As he learned things, he put it all together logically: his father had abandoned his mother for some other silly woman. They both still lived in the same city, the very place that the betrayal of his mother had occurred. His plan practically sprang to life fully developed. He moved there and set up a post office box so he could receive his weekly checks from the modest inheritance that had been left him.

The rest was easy: painstakingly methodical, but easy. He proudly envisioned himself as a kind of ninja secret agent, slipping in and out of both their lives undetected. He had been right under their noses. Sometimes they had actually seen him and passed by him without a clue that he was their righteous nemesis.

He had learned all about them, starting with the woman, his father's silly harlot: there was something about her, some kind of vibration he could sense, that told him her innermost secrets. She was emotionally unsteady, he could feel it. Not surprising in such an evil presence, he judged. Evil was always, at heart, weak. He began to subtly work on her perceived weakness, to leave her deliberately obscure phone messages suggesting her husband was not what he seemed and so forth. Sure enough, she began to come apart.

That was his first objective: to sow torment, confusion and insecurity. When she moved out of the condo, as he knew she would, his plan kicked into the next gear. He followed her to her new apartment and set himself up close by, then approached the building managers and talked them into giving him a job. Again he played his role to perfection. He charmed them into trusting him, making it simple to slip into their quarters and get the keys to the garden apartment.

So began his campaign to undermine her completely, slipping into her place, conspicuously breaking and moving things like some vengeful poltergeist. Finding the photographs was an extra reward for him. He had spent a dangerously long time paging through those — always wearing his latex gloves, of course; he was always smart and careful — before he left them out as a message. Mementos from the past, from the time when she stole his father from his mother. Whether she grasped the message or not was irrelevant. Leaving them out was the whole point.

Getting into his father's place was a bit trickier, but he had been smart and careful there too. He learned the flow of the occupants and followed his father (a man of exacting habit, fortunately, and very predictable) until he knew his schedule down cold. He could predict when the floor was empty, the coast clear, and began to perform subtle mischiefs, escalating as he proceeded. He especially enjoyed poisoning the dog. He had never liked dogs.

Then came the long-awaited endgame. He stepped up his campaign against his father's silly harlot until, as he had predicted, she fled her apartment in terror. He was watching her diligently, easily followed her to the hotel, and realized everything was in place. It was time for the culmination of his smart and careful plan.

He made a quick call to his father and said simply, 'I'm your son. I'm coming over to tell you the story.' He knew the twelfth floor was deserted and would remain so for long enough. His father opened the door without hesitation. His one regret was that he had instantly died from the Taser gun: he had hoped to simply stun him, drag him in, and finish the job with his garotte, then perhaps search for photos or memorabilia. But brilliant planners improvise, after all.

He wore gloves, left no prints, left only the note he had printed out the night before on one of the computers available at an instant printer. He purposely left the door ajar and fled when he heard the elevator doors open. Someone was coming home early.

By this time he began to work himself into a rage. Something about the living purity of his anger, the newness and the intensity of it, actually felt good to him. He savored it, letting it build and build as he drove to the hotel.

He knocked on the harlot's door, saying he was a maintenance person, and the stupid woman let him right in! His fury was so pure and fierce, it was hard to remember what followed. But he knew he had been smart and careful. He had even waited long enough to undo the cord and leave the note. This time he had hand-printed it. Different but similar. That would throw them off. And he thought it a nice touch to leave the maid sign on the door as he departed.

He had a wonderful, reassuring clarity about everything. The authorities were stupid, he was smart. By the time they figured out anything, he would be long gone. All he needed was the last check. No notice or farewells to anyone; he would just leave. He would pack his car tonight.

So why was he trembling uncontrollably?

He turned off the television and considered the terrible anxiety clawing at his insides. Once he was on the road, away from this monstrous city that had destroyed his mother and his life, maybe it would all start to feel better.

Maybe his check had come yesterday and he could leave sooner, cash it somewhere on the road. He hadn't checked the mail this weekend. The area with the lock boxes was usually left open by the post office on the weekends.

Maybe it was worth going over to check it out. Perhaps what was driving him crazy was the inaction, the waiting. He decided to walk over right now. At the very least it was something to do, to occupy his time.

9

Frank had only seen him one time for just a few moments, but Emil looked as he remembered him from that brief encounter: lean but muscular, short dark hair, clean shaven: a fairly ordinary-looking young man in dark shirt and jeans. Downright nondescript.

He may have deliberately avoided any physical characteristics, like a beard or mustache that would make him noticeable. He was leaving his apartment house, a low brick building on a narrow street in a neighborhood one would hardly describe as upscale. Frank had just parked his car across the street when he saw Emil coming out the doorway directly onto the sidewalk, turning to his right. He seemed to be preoccupied, taking long strides without paying much heed to his surroundings.

Frank looked up and down the street. No officer backup yet. He couldn't wait. He was out of the car, on his feet and calculating an angle to cross the street and intercept his quarry. He reached under his jacket pocket to the service automatic he kept in his shoulder holster and kept his hand there as he walked.

Emil was still seemingly oblivious to his immediate environment, walking fast. Frank checked the street for traffic and began to cross, angling in on him.

Suddenly there was the squeal of brakes and a blare of a car horn. Frank looked up to see a car pulling out of a parking space driven by a young woman who had been looking in her mirror, not to her front. She was just about to accelerate right into him before seeing him at the last minute, and now she was yelling something at him.

Frank cursed under his breath. He looked up to see Emil, about ten feet away, staring right at him. For a moment he froze as they looked at each other. Recognition dawned in the young man's eyes and he turned to run.

Hang the luck. He hated chases. He yelled out, 'Hey Emil! Hang on! I just want to talk to you!' even as he broke into a dash as best he could. He wasn't kidding himself here.

Emil had at least a couple of decades on him and he didn't think he had much of a chance of catching him in a chase. He was going to lose him and probably never find him again, now that he had been tipped off. The advantage would be forever lost.

He could see Emil expanding the distance between them even as they raced down the block, and he thought he heard sirens not far away. Frank considered drawing his weapon and announcing he would shoot if Emil did not stop. He knew Emil would not stop and he would have to shoot. In the split second before he made his decision, fate intervened.

The way Frank would later tell the story: 'Well, not exactly fate — it was a squad car that intervened.'

At the intersection, Emil shot into the street, not slowing his pace or looking in either direction. There was a scream of brakes. Frank, bringing himself to an abrupt stop, could not help but see Emil Benecke flying up onto the blue and white hood of a police cruiser that was screeching to a halt on the pavement.

Suddenly Frank was very much aware that there were indeed sirens, and they were all around him.

10

'Lucky perp,' Lieutenant Castillo was remarking. 'He could have been badly injured, even killed.' His voice suggested that he wasn't exactly relieved at this turn of fate.

There were those cynics among the force who would have happily suggested that such a course would have been preferable, saving the city an expensive trial and ensuring that justice had indeed been served. Frank was not one of those.

'A few bumps and scratches, some bandages. I'd say he was lucky indeed. Me too. I was about to draw my weapon on him. I knew that if he got away from me, he would be in the wind for good.'

Castillo nodded seriously. 'Always a bad thing when you have to fire your weapon, especially if it's fatal. And in the back, that's worse. Inquests, all sorts of stuff; put you on leave while it's investigated, all that.'

Not to mention, thought Frank, *the death of another human being on my shoulders*. It would not have been the first death at his hands, and the odds were such that it would not be the last. Sometimes it had been utterly necessary. That unfortunately came with his job. But he didn't want another one if he could help it. Certainly not this way. It seemed to him that Castillo felt differently.

'Is he talking?' Castillo asked.

Frank shrugged. 'He said he didn't want a lawyer. I guess he thinks he's smarter than any of them. My guess is he'll talk before long, and my other guess is he's going to be found mentally unsound.'

★　★　★

Frank turned out to be correct on both counts. Emil Benecke would tell his tale and a court would find him unfit to stand trial. The entire far-fetched scenario would gradually come to light and cause more than one detective to shake their head in amazement.

Emil would ultimately be remanded to an institution for the remainder of his life, with no chance of ever seeing the outside world again. Ultimately, all those left behind would find some kind of closure in their own lives.

Once he did begin to talk, Emil wouldn't shut up. He insisted that the world know his story. He dictated a lengthy manifesto to his interrogators. Everything to him had a logic that he said was 'glaringly clear.'

When he was asked about his choice of weapons, Emil was forthright. His grandfather had died by electrocution. Somehow he had come to believe that his mother had suffocated to death in childbirth. He also had come to see the disappointments of his own life in terms of being suffocated and then shocked. He said there was a 'symmetry' that Max and Margo should die by electrocution and strangling.

A search of Emil's residence turned up the Taser, an impressive set of locksmith's tools and picks, and even a set of Sharpie permanent markers, the kind that had been used to create the note left on

Margo Hesterberg's body. It would have been a slam-dunk case for any prosecutor, Frank would later consider, excepting for the fact that the defendant was totally bonkers.

* * *

Frank decided he had a few more loose ends to tie up on the cases before moving on. As he left Castillo's office, he passed Marlon Morrison, who gave him a pat on the back and said, 'Great job, Frank. I knew I gave that to the right guy.'

Frank couldn't help noticing that Marlon was carrying a thick and familiar file and wasn't looking very happy as he trudged to his desk.

* * *

'The coroner will release the body tonight,' Monica said. They were once again sitting in her front parlor, this time with cups of tea on the table in front of them. 'Thank you for all your help, Detective. Will you be at the memorial service day after tomorrow?'

'I'm not sure, Ms. Wersching. Demands of the job and all. I'll try to be there though.' In reality he hoped to avoid either service, now that the cases had been resolved. There was something about all these people that bothered him.

Earlier that day he had talked to Angie Colletta on the phone and conveyed basically the same answer that he would try to make the services for Max but might not be able to be present.

They talked briefly about Max and his memory, and then he had asked her about Gary Rossi. Specifically he was curious: why had she neglected to mention him in their own conversation but then had referred him to Frank after the fact?

'Well, can I level with you, Detective?'

'Sure.'

'I had these memories of Gary, you know? From when I was much younger and a student. And he was this kind of flirty, hunky older guy, the whole working man thing with the tool belt and all. I kind of thought maybe I could look him up and see if he resembled my memories.'

'Uh huh,' mumbled Frank, rubbing the back of his neck.

'He wasn't that hard to find. Still in the book.' She paused, probably to take a puff from her cigarette, and continued in her throaty voice. 'Frank — may I call you that? Because I find this hard to say if I'm calling you Detective. Frank, I gotta tell you, me and my longtime hubby, we have kinda grown apart just a little. Here I was stuck here for who knows how long; I'm bored and restless, are you following me? I just thought I'd look into him, what was the harm?'

He contributed another 'Uh huh,' as if he were monitoring a confession in an interview room. It was feeling like that all of a sudden.

'Well, I met up with him, and let's just say you can't go back, you know?'

'I know.'

'I felt this sudden wave of shame and embarrassment that this old sad, sloppy drunk was the object of my little-girl fantasies and that I was entertaining any ideas, however slight, of fooling around on my Vinnie back home. My life's not perfect, but it's actually not bad, you know? And I suddenly missed my job and my guy. So I told Gary he should get in touch with you and gave him your number; I figured that gave me an excuse and an out. And I got the hell out of that shoddy bar.'

'I bet I even know which bar.'

'Sorry to inflict him on you.'

'No, actually he was of value.'

'We all should be, Frank,' Angie coughed. 'We all should be.'

He snapped back to the present and realized he had missed the beginning of what Monica was telling him.

' . . . so I think maybe once that's done I might move on.'

'I'm sorry,' Frank said a bit sheepishly. The observant, ever-vigilant detective, caught daydreaming. He shook his head as if to clear the cobwebs, causing Monica to smile. 'Did you say you're leaving town?'

'As soon as Margo's put to rest and her things are put in order. There are too many bad memories here and no real reason for me to stay. I'll keep a few of her mementoes and, as I said, move on.'

'Where will you go?'

'I'm not sure. I've got money saved. Maybe it's time for an adventure, a new town and a new beginning. I got to thinking that Margo and I tended to sit around way too much. Maybe I can travel, then find a place with some part-time or volunteer work with someone not afraid to take on an elderly lady like me.'

'You're not that old,' Frank said.

'I'm ancient,' Monica laughed. 'But that won't stop me.' Then she changed the subject. 'That demented lunatic man,' she said sadly. 'I feel bad for him, even after what he did. He must have been so tortured inside.'

'The whole story may never come out. It seems his step-parents did the best they could, but they were sort of loopy to begin with. And they never told him the truth about his real mother.'

'He played upon my sister's insecurities. He drove her to a kind of insanity, as much as I didn't want to believe that, and destroyed her marriage. I ended up hating Max too. That — monster — destroyed us all. I should want to watch this Emil Benecke drawn and quartered.' She looked up at Frank, her chin high in a curious pose of nobility. 'But I don't. I'm angry, yes, but mostly I just feel this horrible pity for him. Isn't that strange?'

'No, it just proves your humanity, Monica.'

They chatted a bit further. Frank took a last sip of tea, thanked her for the refreshments, stood up and wished her good luck. As he walked out the door he knew he would likely never see her, or Angela Colletta, again. That was all for the best.

By the time he was in his car he was trying his best to flush away his uncomfortable feelings from the Hesterberg cases. He had dealt with much worse, and had always walked away from those cases with some vestige of sanity if not serenity. This one would pass, too. He tried to shift his brain to the other cases awaiting his return to his desk.

A human being's seemingly unlimited

potential for inhumanity never ceased to affect him, he reflected. Moving on and leaving the demons behind was never easy, and sometimes he didn't entirely succeed. But as he had just advised Monica Wersching, perhaps that just proved his humanity.

THE CLASSIC CAR KILLER

Richard A. Lupoff

The members of the New California Smart Set love to dress in the fashions of the 1920s and dance to the music of that bygone era. They even bring out a magnificent vintage limousine for display at their annual gala — which is promptly stolen. Insurance investigator Hobart Lindsey is called upon to unravel an intricate puzzle that soon leads to brutal murder and an attempt on his own life. Aided by his streetwise police officer girlfriend Marvia Plum, the unlikely partners are off on another hazardous adventure!

GRAVE WATERS

Ana R. Morlan and Mary W. Burgess

Two cunning, cold-blooded killers board the cruise ship *Nerissa* disguised as an elderly couple, with a deadly armoury at their disposal courtesy of the Russian Mafia. Meanwhile, members of a mysterious cult called the Foundation have infiltrated the passenger list, with their own sinister agenda to take over the ship. When they strike, they disrupt the on-board wedding ceremony of police officer David Spaulding. Can the ship's captain, aided by David and his new friend, author and anthropologist Richard Black Wolf, regain control of the *Nerissa* before it's too late?

THE OTHER MRS. WATSON

Michael Mallory

Who was the elusive second wife of John Watson, trusted friend and chronicler of the great Sherlock Holmes? The secret is now revealed in *The Other Mrs. Watson*, eight stories featuring Amelia Watson, devoted and opinionated wife of the good doctor, and intrepid (if a bit reluctant) amateur sleuth. Jack the Ripper is back, and up to his old tricks . . . Ghosts and demons materialise to trouble the living . . . An old acquaintance of Holmes's reappears, with cut-throats on her tail . . . And murder seems to lurk around every corner!

MISSION: THIRD FORCE

Michael Kurland

In the late 1960s, the Cold War threatens the survival of mankind. To help keep the uneasy peace, a new group of mercenaries is born: known as Weapons Analysis and Research, Incorporated. Whilst WAR, Inc. does not supply fighting troops, it provides training, equipment, systems, advice and technical expertise ... Now former major Peter Carthage leads his men into the hostile jungles of Bonterre to prevent the overthrow of its government by guerillas — and the mysterious Third Force known only as 'X' ...

WEDDINGS ARE MURDER AND OTHER STORIES

Geraldine Ryan

When DI Casey Clunes visits Oakham Manor with a view to holding her wedding there, the last thing she expects to discover is a body. Planning her big day quickly takes second place to solving a murder ... A woman disappears from her family home in mysterious circumstances — but are the grieving family victims, or villains? And what is so important about the contents of some old love letters, that their now-famous author will go to any lengths to stop them being made public?